OL' SHEP
BOOK 1: FAITHFUL SHEP

Ol' Shep: Book 1: Faithful Shep
by Don Denevi
Published by Creative Texts Publishers
PO Box 50
Barto, PA 19504
www.creativetexts.com

ISBN: 978-0-578-47350-5

OL' SHEP

CREATIVE TEXTS PUBLISHERS
Barto, Pennsylvania

For Carrie . . .

… in the backyard, basking in the warmth of the sun alongside Shep, Blackie, and Boots …

"He had been there alone for fifteen days. His side of bacon was eaten, and the sack of corn getting very low. The Rangers were as much delighted as if it had been a human being they had rescued. He had worn the top of the wall of the old stage stand perfectly smooth, standing off the sneaking coyotes … Shep had held the fort.…"

—George Wythe Baylor, Captain (Ret.), Company C, Frontier Battalion, *El Paso Herald*, February 3, 1900

Author's Note

Faithful Shep was written as a tribute arising from admiration of that great daring that is bred in bravery. I dedicate this book to all who ennoble with loving care the warm-hearted animals who revere them in return. May this story of a stranded, starving dog and the ordinary men who trekked into hostile country to save him, serve as a source of inspiration and resolve.

I express sincere appreciation and deep indebtedness to the host of Texas university researchers, reference librarians, and historical archivists whom I continually pestered for details of setting and geography, personal letters from the period, old newspaper clippings, documents on the Texas Rangers, and other minutia that I cannot even recall at the moment. These longsuffering aides to my quest are too numerous to name, but I am thankful they know who they are and that they helped a hero dog live again, briefly, in these pages.

Two names must be mentioned, though. First, I will forever be grateful to Paul Ruffin (1941–2016), former Texas Poet Laureate and director of Texas Review Press. He believed in Shep even more than I did. Second, I thank Thom Lemmons, who edited this manuscript. I hope one day he will forgive the thin quality of the writing that he had to work with.

Don DeNevi

Menlo Park, California

September 2016

TABLE OF CONTENTS

PROLOGUE

-

The dog scented the cougar before he could see it. One of the loud men with stinking breath looped a rope around the dog's neck and pulled him out of the dark shed with the other dogs, toward the high, walled pen, and the dog could smell the big cat behind the wall. He didn't want to go toward danger, but the man had a rope around his neck and wanted him to come.

Long ago, in a time the dog barely remembered, he had been taught by a man who was kind to him. The man taught the dog that he should always obey what humans said. That was before the man had gone away, leaving the dog alone. In the many hungry days since, the dog had to get food wherever he could, had to sleep in dark corners out of the wind wherever they could be found. There had been no one to feed the dog, to teach him what to do, or to tell him where to go.

Then, one of the bad-smelling men found the dog and brought him to this place with other dogs. They all stayed in a dark shed until one of the men came to bring one of the dogs outside, to the pen where the mountain lion waited. None of the other dogs had ever come back. Now, one of the men had come for the dog, and he was going toward the high-walled pen.

The dog walked beside the bad-smelling man, and the pen got closer and closer. And even though the dog had obeyed the man and had not tried to pull back or run away, when they reached the gate to the pen, the man shoved him roughly inside and kicked him, as if the dog had done something wrong. Then the man slammed the gate shut.

The mountain lion was crouched against the wall opposite the gate, staring at the dog, its ears flattened and its teeth bared in a snarl. The dog could smell the cougar's fright, its rage. He could see the muscles bunching in the cat's hindquarters and shoulders as it prepared to spring.

The dog was hungry and weak, because the bad-smelling men had given him nothing to eat. The pads of his right forefoot were raw and bleeding. He looked around, searching in terror for a way out, a place to run. But there was no way out. There was nothing except the dog, the panicked, vicious cougar, and the bloody, lifeless remains of the other dogs that had been dragged in here by the loud, bad-smelling men. The dog's tail curled under his body; he dropped his head and turned his eyes away, to show that he didn't want to fight. He released the contents of his bladder into the dust of the pen, helpless with fear.

The yelling of the men outside the walls got louder. The dog was scared and confused. His senses were assaulted on all sides by the smell of old blood, the stink of his own fear, the acrid odor of the cougar, the noise of the men. A whimper started, deep down in the dog's throat.

The cougar outweighed the dog; it was bigger and stronger. The dog feared the cougar's claws and teeth. He did not want to fight the cougar; he had no chance. But the cougar was scared and angry. It would attack—and soon.

There was another noise behind the dog, more yelling. Then the gate slammed open and another man was inside the pen. He was standing beside the dog, and then he was kneeling. He spoke in a quiet, soothing tone—something no human had done with him in a very long time. The man's hands were gentle on the dog and his voice was low.

The cougar was still staring at them, still preparing to charge, but now, because the man was there, it hesitated. The man kept talking, and then the dog knew he would go with the man. The man stood up and started moving back toward the gate, and the dog went with him. He and the man backed carefully toward the gate; they watched the cougar, and the cougar watched them, but it did not attack.

They reached the gate, and another man was there. Like the man who had come into the pen, he did not smell of the foulness that stank on the breath of most of the other men who gathered around the tall enclosure to yell and fight and take dogs into the pen. The two men closed the gate. They kept the dog between them, and the three of them walked past the other, bad-smelling men, most of whom had suddenly become quiet. Many of them were looking at the ground or somewhere else, the way the dog had looked away from the cougar. The man who had come into the pen was angry; the dog could sense it. But he was not angry at the dog. No, he was angry at the loud men, the ones who were standing around the outside of the pen.

The dog and the two men walked away from the pen with the high walls, and the more they walked, the less afraid the dog felt. The two men talked to him in low, quiet voices; their hands were kind.

They went to another place, and there the two men gave the dog food and clean water to drink. They cleaned the wounds in his pads and wrapped his foot so that it could heal and stop hurting. Soon, he could again walk without limping.

The dog was glad to be with someone again—someone who did not smell foul and who was not loud or always fighting. The two men would talk to him and tell him things. They fed him every day and made sure he had water. He was with them now, and he was not scared anymore. The dog would go wherever they went. He would do whatever the two men told him to do.

CHAPTER ONE

-

By the time Joseph P. Andrews and William Wiswall rode into San Antonio on that afternoon in the early fall of 1879, they had already covered some 1,000 miles of rough, dry, and dusty country. They traversed southern Colorado, from their starting point in the mining country of Ouray County, and made their way across the Indian Territory before crossing the Red River into Texas. And even though they had come this far already, they were still many weary miles and, likely, several negotiations away from the goal of their quest.

Still, this fledgling city at the spring-fed headwaters of the San Antonio River was a welcome sight. The heat was unusually stifling for this time of the year; their horses plodded forward with heads down, and Shep, the black German Shepherd who was their constant companion, trotted along in his usual position, twenty feet ahead. It was early afternoon on Sunday, and both men were hungry and in need of beer. Doubtless, their mounts wanted hay, and Shep would probably be content with a bowl of milk and a beef bone.

Slumped in their saddles, Andrews and Wiswall scrutinized their surroundings. San Antonio was the principal trading post for hundreds of miles in this part of the vast border region of Texas, and the streets brimmed with hustling men and wagons, the wheels creaking under their loads. Vaqueros from surrounding ranchos rode past or lolled at street corners, laughing and conversing with señoritas who hurried by, carrying baskets of corn or buckets of water.

The bustle enveloped the two as they rode into town. In this northern section of the city, home-grown foodstuffs glutted stalls along the streets, the prices low compared to the markets in Denver. To the two mining engineers, the whole of the American Southwest seemed bent on showing its wares in these busy dirt roads and avenues. Street corner hawkers cried for buyers for their vegetables, fruits, berries, grapes, nuts, and eggs.

But it was the people who most captured the attention of the partners. Most of the denizens of this street appeared young, tight-lipped, and dusty. None wore a gun.

Sombreroed braceros trundled barrows past sauntering soldiers from newly built Fort Sam Houston. Cowboys mingled with tradesmen, merchants, and teamsters. Carretas and water wagons trundled past, drawn by horses or burros..

"Saloons and cantinas up and down the street," Wiswall observed, "but not a ragged, unshaved person or stumbling drunkard in sight. Too busy, I guess. Or too much to do."

"Could be," Andrews said, nodding. "From what I heard tell back in Oklahoma, more than a hundred people are coming from the east to Texas every day. It doesn't look like they're turning anyone away in San Antone."

As they made their way through San Antonio, dogs occasionally approached Shep: some with raised hackles and stiff-legged walks and others with wagging tails and extended noses. The black shepherd received all comers with due caution or good humor, as the occasion warranted. His ears stayed tilted forward, his nostrils flaring in and out. Shep was clearly as absorbed in this unfamiliar place as the men were.

Nearing the center of town, the swarms of people, horses, and stray dogs thinned out. Along these thoroughfares, all of the two- and three-story buildings were constructed of brick or wood frame. A few adobe structures remained in between. Whereas the outskirts had housed a saloon or cantina in every third or fourth building, not one was now seen. All the wide avenues were lined with shiny new rails where saddled horses and teams hitched to clean wagons and buggies. Since it was afternoon on a Sunday, vested, cravated businessmen and a few well-dressed women enjoyed an after-lunch stroll before returning home from church services.

"Remember what the sheriff in Austin told us?" asked Wiswall.

"You mean that business about how they stack bricks of gold and silver on the sidewalks outside the banks?" laughed Andrews. "I also remember that he wasn't sure if that was here or in El Paso. He might have had one or two of his facts crossed.”

“Maybe we ought to plan a robbery.”

“Hew to the line, friend and partner. Any gold and silver we get will come from selling a string of packing burros back up in Ouray County—once we can find and buy them, that is.”

Wiswall chuckled.

Past the first-class hotels and restaurants they rode, Shep pacing steadily in front. There were establishments holding themselves out as manufacturers of jewelry and importers of diamonds, lumber distributors (“Oak, Hickory, Pine, and Redwood for Shingles, Sash, and Doors—Terms Available to Reputable Parties”), and wholesale and retail druggists’ offices. They passed physicians’ and surgeons’ residences; attorney-at-law offices; liveries and saddlers; a commercial college; national banks; a livestock yard; a merchant offering pianos, organs, and coffins; dry goods stores; and sales offices for liquors by the case and Mexican cigars. There were soap and tallow outlets; dentists; marble works; offices for the sale of mineral rights; and vendors of crockery, china, glassware, house furnishing, books and stationery, sewing machines … There seemed no end to the commercial enterprises under pursuit by the good people of San Antonio.

“Where should we stay tonight?” said Wiswall.

"I'm game for that hotel on the plaza. It looks brand-new, and the sign out front said it opened only last week. We can get supper right across the street."

"That's fine. Do you reckon they'll allow Shep to sleep in our room?"

"He'll not likely sleep anywhere else."

And so it was that the two men from Colorado decided to room at the American House Hotel. By morning they hoped to decide whether Corpus Christi, Brownsville, Laredo, Eagle Pass, or some other place beneath the Lone Star held the best prospects for their planned purchase of pack burros to satisfy the need of the burgeoning mining enterprises back in Ouray County. With a good supper tucked behind their belts and some scraps fed to Shep, Andrews and Wiswall would canvass the opinions of the dozen or so men sitting on the hotel's veranda, enjoying their evening pipes.

The American House Hotel was a three-story brick structure situated at one corner of the city center. Standing on the street in front of the gleaming new establishment, Andrews and Wiswall gazed upon the edifice with respect. On their journey through Colorado and the Oklahoma and Indian Territories into Texas, they had often slept in crude log huts or even canvas accommodations. But the American House was built of imported bricks, not adobe. It was a structure of substance and looked to the two weary travelers like the Taj Mahal.

After securing permission for Shep to enter the hotel and sleep in their room, Andrews and Wiswall registered at the desk, paid $2.00 for a room with bath, and escorted Shep to a blanket on the floor of their quarters. They bathed and then changed their clothes for supper. Then, they made a quick check of the small barn attached to the rear of the hotel, satisfying themselves that their horses were unsaddled, brushed down, watered, and getting fed.

Since there was still at least an hour's worth of daylight, they strolled around the long blocks surrounding and enclosing the city center before entering Link's Restaurant.

Andrews was the taller and more slender of the two. Wiswall, though shorter and a bit more stout, was solidly built. Both of them were accustomed to physical labors in the out-of-doors; neither had any difficulties obtaining and keeping the respect of the persons they customarily dealt with, be they miners with hardened hands and creased faces, or mine owners dressed in linen and seated amid leather upholstery and mahogany paneling.

The two strolled easily along, stopping to chat with shopkeepers, clerks, and patrons they met along the way. They encountered husbands and wives, arm in arm, with children tagging along behind; farmers and ranchers in business suits; and military men in recently pressed uniforms. Yet, everywhere they looked, they noted incongruities: music from a hurdy-gurdy sounding from a gambling den deep within one of the old buildings facing the center of the square;

loud laughter and noisy talk from every other open window; an Indian man and his squaw squatted against the wall outside an expensive jewelry store. After their rambling walk, Andrews and Wiswall finally stood before the restaurant.

"Are you fellows new to town?" a passerby said to the two. When they told him they were, he informed them, "Well, you won't find a better chop house anywhere around than Link's. It might be the best eatery in all of Texas."

They paused in the doorway to survey the interior. The entire facility was stylish; clearly, the place catered to San Antonio's powerful and well-to-do. An elaborate rosewood bar ran the length of the wall on their left, all the way to a small alcove over a raised stage with footlights. Large mirrors of Spanish plate reflected light into the room. Some twenty-five tables, each seating four patrons, sat at comfortable distances from one another. Crystal goblets and glasses of all shapes and sizes glittered on tables and in waiting pyramids at one end of the bar. The floor was of varnished hardwood. Oil lamps with reflectors shed a buttery glow throughout the room. To the two hard-riding partners from Ouray County, Colorado, the effect was palatial.

The travelers were disappointed, though, to see that all the tables were occupied. A compact group of about six lingered near the center of the bar, and some dozen or so more waited in a vestibule.

Andrews and Wiswall walked to the back of the line in the vestibule, resigned to waiting for their turn. There, at the end of the line, a middle-aged man of military bearing nodded at them.

"Shouldn't be too long," he offered.

Neatly dressed, he was thin-haired, with leathery, well-tanned skin that started below the stark white hat-brim line just above his eyebrows.

"I'm Joseph Andrews, and this is my partner, William Wiswall. We are just down from Ouray County, Colorado." Andrews took the other man's hand in a firm, dry grip. "We're rooming for the night over at the American House."

"Well, us and our dog," Wiswall added, chuckling.

"Good to know you," the man said, loosing his grip on Andrews's hand to take Wiswall's in turn. "I'm Charley Nevill, and I'd offer you a place to bunk, but I'm afraid I'm camping on the river."

The group in front of the three men took a few steps forward, and they followed along behind. It seemed to Andrews and Wiswall that their new acquaintance was correct in his assessment of their imminent seating at a table.

"You a cattleman?" asked Wiswall. "You have the look of a man who has spent a fair share of his time out in the weather."

"Well, that I have, but I'm not much in the cattle line, no."

"Perhaps you can help us," Wiswall said. "We're looking to buy a hundred or more packing burros to trail back to Colorado." The line moved forward another several paces.

"No, boys, I'm afraid I can't advise you. I'm new to this part of Texas, myself."

"I see. Well, what sort of work is it that you do?" Andrews said.

"I'm a Texas Ranger."

Just then, the maitre'd of the restaurant approached. "Gentlemen, I have a side-window table that can seat three, if you squeeze a bit. Do you want it?"

Andrews and Wiswall shrugged and nodded, then looked at Nevill. "Yes, I believe my friends and I will take the table," the Ranger said, smiling. The maitre'd led them to a small, half-round table abutting a window overlooking the city center.

After perusing the offerings, all three decided upon the restaurant's Sunday house specialty, as prominently advertised on the front of the menu's four-page fold-out:

Sunday specialty of Link's—dinner soup, clam chowder; meat, roast pork with green apple sauce; entrée, macaroni and cheese, chicken salad; dessert, tapioca-apple pudding; pastry, summer mince pie and currant cake; coffee, milk, or tea. No alcoholic beverages sold in the dining room.

As they waited for their food to arrive, Andrews and Wiswall learned that their new acquaintance was 2nd Lt. Charles L. Nevill, acting commanding officer of Company E, Texas Rangers. He had been leading the company less than two weeks. Headquartered at Fort Davis, far to the west, his assigned district covered both Pecos and Presidio counties.

Nevill further related that his good friend, Pvt. William Harris of Company B, had been killed during an Apache raid at the head of the North Concho River in July, and Lieutenant Nevill was in San Antonio with the sad duty of calling upon the man's family.

"I am sorry to hear of the loss of your friend," Andrews said. Wiswall nodded.

"Harris was a good friend and a fine Ranger. He volunteered for many of my expeditions. I owe him a great debt; calling personally upon his relatives is the least I can do."

Dinnerwas a delight. Andrews and Wiswall enjoyed the lieutenant and his conversation. As they ate, Nevill predicted that a welcome, cleansing rain would soon be upon them, and abundantly so, since virtually the entire southwest was due after three years of inordinate, excessive heat and drought.

"You fellows ought to see how a good rain can transform the deserts and prairies. No Texan ever complains about rain. Even the Apaches will tell you it's coming—and in buckets."

"The Indians set great store by the weather, then?" Andrews said.

Nevill nodded as he speared a morsel of pork. "Rain, in their thinking, is witchery; it brings life to dryness, to all that grows and breathes, and to men themselves."

"We don't have a force like the Rangers up in Colorado," Wiswall said, a bit later. "Police, sheriffs, and posses, for sure, but no lawmen just rambling around the country. What kind of men are you and your fellow Rangers?"

Nevill took a long, slow sip of his coffee. He gave his companions a careful look.

"Five years ago, I served under Capt. L. H. McNelly in a special company of Rangers dispatched to settle some trouble in DeWitt County. In those days, we were so poor that we had to beg for ammunition and horseshoes. But we did what we had to do.

"There were some fellows down there who were hell-bent on continuing to fight the Civil War, you see. And they attracted all the wrong sort of rough men to their cause. But when we went down there, and we finally put a stop to it."

"What did you have to do?" Andrews asked.

Nevill fixed him with a steady, green-eyed gaze. "Whatever it took."

After a pause, he continued his narration. "After calming the troubles there, Captain McNelly was asked to form Company A of the organization, and I signed up for it, too. We entered hellhole after hellhole, rooting out the worst of the worst, criminals of every persuasion. I never knew, heard of, or served with such a true and faithful commander.

"And so, to answer your original question … What sort of fellows are the Texas Rangers? We're the sort who will do what we must, at any time, to keep order in the state and to make it safe for law-abiding citizens. We will take on any fight, and we will see it through to the end, by whatever means are at hand."

Nevill studied the gold locket dangling from Andrews's neck. "What does the locket signify, Mr. Andrews?" asked Nevill, presently. "It must mean something to you, since you don't see men wearing them much."

Andrews, without looking up from his coffee cup, answered, "You are correct, sir. It's not a simple memento or a mere piece of jewelry. This locket contains a snippet of my mother's and my father's hair. I lost my parents six years ago. My dearest hope is that one day, I'm laid to rest next to them in Austin."

"If you will permit me a personal inquiry, how did they die?" Nevill said.

"Kiowa and Comanche raiders ambushed them at their homestead, just before the start of the Red River Wars."

"I am very sorry," Nevill said. "I believe the army finally put all that to rights a few years back, but I suppose it was too late for your folks."

Andrews nodded. "It happened just after I left home for the mining country in Colorado. I have carried a burden of guilt ever since."

Wiswall said quietly, "Lieutenant, I daresay the decent folk of Texas owe a great debt to you Rangers. I hope you receive the appreciation you ought to have."

Nevill smiled. "Well, we don't serve for the appreciation. It is thanks enough to see the country governed by law and hospitable to the honest efforts of good, enterprising people. But now and then, someone offers a few words of gratitude, and that is awfully nice to hear, I'll admit."

Nevill reached behind him, into a pocket of the short jacket hanging on the back of his chair. He withdrew a much-handled, often-folded page from a newspaper.

"A schoolmarm from Brenham, a day's ride northeast of here, wrote up a pretty little tribute, not too long ago. It found its way into one of the newspapers, and I keep it with me. Sometimes, when my comrades and I are on a long ride, I'll take this out and read it over again, in the light of the campfire, just to remind myself of why we Rangers do what we do. Would you like to hear it?"

After Andrews and Wiswall gave their encouragement, Nevill cleared a place on the table and spread the newsprint in front of him. "She calls it, 'The Texas Rangers,'" he said, and started reading.

It was indeed a lovely piece of encomium. It described the Ranger as he might be situated on a long patrol: astride a sturdy mount, wrapped in an oilskin slicker or a woolen blanket against the cold and wet, tirelessly trailing a band of marauding Indians, or a gang of border desperadoes, or a wily criminal bent on victimizing a remote settlement. The article discussed the early days of the organization: the times when the newly formed territory of Texas was rapidly gaining a reputation for crime, desperation, and massacre. Hence, volunteer companies were organized for protection. These were the first soldiers to be called Rangers.

The piece lauded the bravery of the Rangers, describing how they served without uniforms, took part in no parades, and even avoided the congress of throngs. Rather, they spent their days in the saddle, their nights in the open, pursuing evildoers wherever they might be found and bringing them to justice.

When Nevill finished reading, a lengthy silence followed. Finally, Wiswall, looking past his dining companions and through the restaurant's window onto the town center, said quietly, "I am glad you read that, Lieutenant. And I am pleased that some folks in Texas, at least, realize how grateful they should be for the presence of the Texas Rangers." Nevill inclined his head in thanks.

"What are the matters of most concern for you and your fellow Rangers these days, Lieutenant?" said Andrews.

"Of all we contend with currently, we are most worried about the Apache chief Victorio." Seeing the puzzled looks of the men, Nevill continued.

"A few months ago, Victorio and a couple hundred warriors, along with women and children, broke out of their reservation in Arizona Territory and headed into Mexico. Since then, they have been raiding and terrorizing the country from Fort Davis, all the way west to El Paso and into New Mexico. Victorio is as wily as they come, and my friends in the army tell me he is no mean tactician. I talked to a trooper from the Sixth Cavalry who chased him, and he told me that everywhere Victorio went, he left behind murdered, burned bodies, ruined ranches, and slaughtered cattle and sheep."

"Has he been seen in these parts?" Wiswall said.

"Not around here. But the entire western region of Texas, New Mexico, northwestern Mexico, and Arizona are extremely dangerous places. Pity the people he catches, be they Mexican, US citizens, or even Indians not of his own tribe."

After looking at the two Coloradoans for a moment, Nevill said, "Gentlemen, I think that I will give you some advice about your burros, after all. If you can't find what you need in this part of Texas or farther south and east, then just go back home to Ouray County. Don't risk going west of here."

CHAPTER TWO

-

With Lieutenant Nevill's warning ringing in their ears, the partners spent two more days in San Antonio, making inquiries at various liveries and among such persons as they could find who seemed knowledgeable about livestock and where it might be procured. Their hesitancy to leave the creaturely comforts of the American House Hotel encouraged the leisurely pace of their investigation. Though not lacking in skills or nerve—and having provided for themselves a good arsenal of arms against the dangers they anticipated on the trail—they were uncertain of the best direction to take in pursuing their aim of procuring burros.

Ultimately, the duo judged that their best path for the present was as Nevill had suggested; they would point south and east, following the old San Patricio cattle trail that led from San Antonio toward the town founded by Irish immigrants to what was then the northern part of Mexico, nearly fifty years previous, and named for their patron saint. From there, they would strike for the nearby coastal city of

Corpus Christi and follow the coast down to the Mexican border town of Matamoros, across the Rio Grande from Brownsville. They reasoned that by working their way from that point gradually north along the river, continuing through the several cities, towns, and hamlets along its banks on both sides, they were likely to come across an adequate supply of the sort of pack animals they sought. With a sigh as they departed the comforts of San Antonio, Andrews withdrew the currency from his money belt to settle their account at the hotel. They saddled up and rode out of town, bound for San Patricio.

<<line break>>

After a fortnight in the saddle and most nights sleeping under the stars, the two men, with their dog leading the way, finally reached the Rio Grande at the place where it emptied, wide, brown, and flat, into the Gulf of Mexico at the utter tip of the United States of America.

They spent their first night in a hostelry run by Miller, counting themselves fortunate, first, that Shep was once again permitted to sleep in their room, and second, that their room was on the recently constructed third floor of the establishment. The next morning, with Shep trailing along at their heels, they set out for the Matamoros side of the river to begin making inquiries after some burros.

"Where do you reckon we ought to start?" Andrews said as they stepped onto the ferry that would take them across the flowing border between the two nations.

"Well, you're the Harvard man," Wiswall said. "I figured you had a plan."

"You figured wrong, partner. I guess we'll find the first place that looks like a livery and commence there."

"How do you know what a livery looks like in Mexico?"

Andrews stared straight ahead as the ferry pushed off from the Texas side. "I imagine we can follow the smell. That ought to translate pretty easily."

Wiswall chuckled. "You see? I knew you had a plan."

Arriving in front of a likely looking establishment, Andrews, in his best Spanish, asked if there were any pack burros to be had in the vicinity.

The man attending the low-roofed, wooden shed, instead of answering, just stared at Shep, who, standing beside Wiswall, returned the fellow's look with intent interest.

"Sit down, Shep," Wiswall said quietly, and the dog promptly sat. "I think you're making this man nervous."

Looking from Shep to Wiswall, then up to Andrews, the man said, in heavily accented but perfectly understandable words, "Señor, why don't you try again in English? I can't understand you."

As Wiswall covered a smile, Andrews said, "We are looking to buy as many as a hundred burros, suitable for service as pack animals. We have means to make immediate payment for the right kind of stock."

The Mexican man nodded slowly. "A hundred?"

Andrews nodded.

The Mexican nodded a bit more. He studied the ground for a few seconds, then looked up at Andrews. "No, señor. I don't know anybody who has that many burros to sell. But I would buy this dog from you; he seems well-mannered and smart, and I could use him to guard the place."

"Shep isn't for sale," Wiswall said. He touched his hat brim. "We appreciate your time, all the same."

The Mexican nodded again. Andrews tipped his hat, and the two men walked on down the street.

After spending the rest of that day making inquiries on both sides of the river—and not receiving the information they hoped for—Andrews and Wiswall determined that the next day they would turn their path along the broad, turbid stream, hoping that they would meet with better success as they made their way through the borderlands.

Well-worn horse and wagon trails led them through Harlingen, McAllen, and all the settlements in between until they reached Rio Grande City in Starr County. Tents, brush lean-tos, and jacales of mud or adobe dotted both sides of the border on the outskirts of the settlements and along the shallow valleys that extended from the riverbanks. Herds of cattle and flocks of sheep and goats grazed the lush meadows and browsed the low scrub.

As Andrews and Wiswall followed the course of the Rio Grande toward the interior, the heat of the late Texas summer began gradually to yield, even so far south, to the cooler nights of autumn. As often as not, a thin, drizzling rain fell on them during the night, driving the men to the imperfectly waterproofed shelter of their small tent, which they shared with Shep. The horses, unsaddled, stood hobbled outside, heads down, the wet dripping off of them in rivulets into the mud. On the damp mornings following such nights, misty air spread an indistinct gray shroud across the flats of scrub mesquite, cenizo, and catclawas far as their eye could see.

Now and then, when they were lucky, they encountered a rude posada that offered a roof and perhaps, for a few centavos, a meal of mashed frijoles and tortillas cooked on a flat, baked-clay comal heated over mesquite coals.

One evening, as boisterous autumn winds rattled and whistled around the sills of the simple hut they shared with the family of Lorenzo Quintana and his family—in the brush country about halfway between Roma and Bellville—the after-supper talk turned to the travelers' intentions, direction, and destination. When Andrews informed their host that they intended to follow the river until they found someone who could sell them pack animals, the wizened vaquero shook his head slowly.

"No esta bien, señores, to keep going much more up Río Bravo. Not by yourselves. Es muy peligroso⌐⌐."

"Why is that?" Wiswall asked, glancing at Andrews.

"Victorio," the Mexican said, glancing at the door as the word passed his lips, as though he feared that saying the name of the Apache chief would summon him, demon-like, from the darkness surrounding the tiny hacienda. "This man is muy malo. He has killed many: gringos, mexicanos, indios … Even los Rinches—the Rangers—they cannot catch him. They chase him, but he vanishes like smoke on the wind."

"What else do you know of Victorio?" Andrews said, as Quintana took out his belt knife and began, slowly and methodically, to scrape it across a sharpening stone. "Almost since we entered Texas, people have been speaking of him. Where did he come from? Who are his people?"

The vaquero shrugged, his eyes never leaving the blade. Metal rasped on stone a half-dozen times before he said, "Es Apache, los Mescaleros, maybe, or maybe Chiricahua. He and his people were on un reservacion farther to the west, maybe Arizona. I think it was a bad place for them. They left to become asaltantes y ladrónes. Since then, los Rinches in Texas and la milicia in Mexico have chased him, but no one can catch him."

A coal popped on the fire. Shep, dozing with his back to the glow, flinched upward at the noise, but soon put his head back down.

"Well, we've got to buy some burros, so I reckon we'll keep going, all the same," Andrews said after another few seconds of silence. "We'll keep a sharp eye out."

The Mexican continued sharpening his knife, carefully, deliberately. "No esta bien," he said into his thick mustache, without looking up. "Muy peligroso."

Despite their most earnest efforts, by the time they had passed through Laredo they had still not found anyone who could sell them the burros they needed. They traveled on past Eagle Pass and Piedras Negras, and finally reached as far as the yet-unnamed village gathering up around San Felipe Springs—still with no luck. By this time, the year had leaned over into winter, and the weather was increasingly cold, wet, and windy.

Andrews and Wiswall had entered the wild and extravagant country lying in the Big Bend of the Rio Grande. Palisaded promontories alternated with vistas almost unimaginably broad, expanding to the horizon in such vast sweeps that the two travelers wondered how even the Almighty might find them amid the immensity.

On a rare morning when the rain had abated, they rode along the river on a path that took them through a thicket of honey mesquite. The riders were obliged to duck or lean to this side or that as their horses picked their way along the winding trail.

"Where are those wide open spaces you were waxing so eloquent about just the other day?" Andrews said.

Wiswall swore softly and grabbed at his hat as a low-slung branch raked it off his head.

Suddenly Shep halted in front of them, stiffening as the hair between his shoulders bristled to attention. Andrew's and Wiswall's mounts both stopped in their tracks, their ears perked forward and their nostrils sifting the morning air.

Something large lurked in the thicket ahead of them—large enough that it felt no need to keep its presence a secret.

The men heard heavy footfalls on the flinty soil and the snapping of twigs. Andrews reached for his Colt revolver and Wiswall readied the Springfield he carried, drawing it from its saddle scabbard while keeping his eyes locked on the moving underbrush in front of them.

They could see a shape moving through the thicket, treading in no particular hurry toward the very path they were on. More footfalls, and then a long, tawny head came poking through the branches of the honey mesquite, followed by a curving neck and a mounded hump.

A camel stood on the trail in front of them. It slowly turned its head in their direction and gave a low, guttural bawl.

Andrews's horse exploded skyward and came down on all four feet, humped like a tomcat in an alley fight. Then it put its head down and flung its hindquarters into the air. It sunfished like a devil-horse. Andrews pulled leather for all he was worth, but it was no good; he flew one direction, the Colt he had been holding went the other way. He arced through the air and landed on his left shoulder; the wind huffed out of him. His horse, squealing in terror, went banging off through the scrub.

Meanwhile, Wiswall was fighting to stay aboard. His horse began to crow-hop, but he had the presence of mind to haul mightily on one side of the reins, pulling the horse's head around nearly to his knee. The horse began dancing in a tight circle, and Wiswall turned the air blue with curses as he tried to holster his rifle and keep his mount under control at the same time. As all this was going on, Shep barked at the height of his ability.

The camel watched everything that was taking place with an apparent lack of alarm or curiosity.

Wiswall was finally able to get his horse headed back the way they had come, then to slow it enough so that he could dismount and grab the bridle. He held onto the reins, keeping the horse's head turned away from the source of the panic.

"Andrews! Are you all right?"

Andrews groaned as he levered himself into a sitting position. He rubbed his left shoulder. "I think so," he called. "I'm damned lucky my noggin didn't bounce off one of these trees, though. Did you see which way my horse went?"

"No idea. I was somewhat preoccupied."

By this time, the camel had wandered into the scrub on the other side of the trail, headed toward the river for a drink. Shep stared in the direction the beast had gone but made no move to follow it.

Andrews got slowly to his feet. He took careful stock of all his bones and joints, satisfying himself, much to his relief, that nothing appeared to be more than bruised. He scouted around until he located his revolver, and he called Shep to his side. "I'll see how far the horse has gone. Damn that camel and all his tribe."

"If the Arabs show up that belong to him, I'll give them your regards," Wiswall said.

"You do that."

Andrews's horse had left a pretty plain trail of scattered gear and trampled underbrush, so it wasn't long until Andrews came upon the animal, standing in a small clearing with its nose to the ground, cropping the thin grass. When he had straightened the saddle and re-tightened the girth strap, he took up the reins and led the horse back toward the trail where Wiswall waited.

"I reckon we just happened upon a refugee from that little experiment the army conducted, back before the Civil War," Wiswall said as Andrews approached. "They tried using camels out here for a while, thought they might stand the heat and the dry better than horses or mules."

"I think I remember reading something about that, a few years back," Andrews said, massaging his shoulder. "But I surely never expected to be unseated because of a camel in the Texas desert."

"You stayed with him for a couple of hops, at least."

"I never said I was a bronc peeler."

"No, you didn't. Well, here's hoping that's the worst surprise we encounter on this little excursion."

"Easy for you to say; I'm the one with the banged-up shoulder."

"Fair enough."

"Is that damned camel out of the way?"

"Appears so, judging by Shep and the horses. Shall we continue?"

"Lead on. I'll ride drag for a while."

CHAPTER THREE

Andrews and Wiswall slanted northwestward along the slow-moving river, averaging twelve to fifteen miles a day. Each day, it seemed, the weather grew wetter. Once Presidio was behind them, they began to encounter more ranches and haciendas, along with signs of organized cattle operations. Fairly often, they saw riders, either solitary or in groups of no more than three, their saddles rigged for heavy roping. These approached slowly, usually with a carbine held loosely in front of them across the pommel, a finger crooked through the trigger guard. Once they could tell the travelers held only innocent intentions, they typically gave one- or two-word answers when questioned. Their wind-creased faces displayed little curiosity.

Staying close to the river and keeping the Chinati and Sierra Vieja ranges on their right, Andrews and Wiswall rode through endless miles of rough, broken country, dotted with sparse outcroppings of creosote and low-slung juniper. Beneath their slickers, they shrugged under the weight of the near-constant rain, hat brims tilted like drooping plates against the downpour.

Four days out of a hamlet called Gallina, they camped beneath an overhang. From the soot on the low ceiling and the darkened places on the rocky floor, they could tell they weren't the first travelers to shelter there. But there were no signs of recent occupants—human, at least—and it was a relief to gain a night's respite from the relentless tapping of the rain's myriad of tiny mallets. There was even enough headroom for the hobbled horses.

The men made a cold camp; all the wood within a hundred miles was soaked to the core. After knifing open a can of beans and passing it back and forth, they leaned back on their saddles and talked quietly in the early dark of the winter and the rain, their voices barely rising above the constant patter beyond the edge of the sheltering overhang. Shep curled up and fell asleep by the back wall.

"What do you calculate Annie is doing, right about now?" Wiswall said.

"Not pining for you, if that's what you're hoping. I imagine she's got the good sense to find herself a man who won't go riding off through the most godforsaken parts of Texas in the middle of a rainy winter."

"Andrews, you can be cruel when you want to be, do you know that?"

Andrews gave a guilty grin. "I'm sorry, partner. I know you miss her. I would be lonesome too if I had a gal back home."

"Maybe that's what's wrong with you. Maybe a woman's touch would moderate that razor-sharp tongue of yours."

"Or make it worse." Andrews eased himself back against his saddle, trying to find a comfortable resting place for his head. "Well, this is certain, at least: I will feel a whole lot better when two things have happened: when we have had a bath apiece in a tub of warm water, and when we have secured safe passage back at least as far as the upper Pecos country."

"Amen to that. But we won't have any show of either of those until we reach Ysleta and El Paso del Norte. I, for one, am longing to see the lights of that place as a departed soul yearns for the first sight of the Pearly Gates," Wiswall said.

Andrews nodded drowsily. "We've spent enough time in purgatory; that's certain."

Wiswall grinned. "You fancy this purgatory?"

"It certainly isn't heaven. It might be full-fledged hell, though."

"I don't think Old Scratch himself could kindle a fire hereabout," Wiswall said. "They don't make a brimstone that can stand up to this constant cold and wet."

They both jumped as Shep gave a sharp yelp and growl. They stared into the dark beyond the sheltering rim, their fingers on the triggers of their Colts. But neither of them saw anything, and the only sound was the soft, unbroken drumming of the rain.

"He's already asleep again," Andrews said, looking back at Shep.

"Dreaming, then, I reckon."

Andrews nodded. "Back in that pit, from the sound of it."

"Most likely. Poor old fellow."

After a long silence, Andrews said, "Have you ever considered what it might feel like to be trapped, knowing you faced a hopeless fight?"

"I've thought of little else, since we found him," Wiswall said. "And lately, come to think of it, I've wondered what it might be like to be Victorio. Penned on a reservation, hundreds of miles from the country you've been accustomed to roaming as free as the wind. I reckon the feeling might be something similar."

Andrews grunted and nodded. "And women and children with him."

After another long spell, Wiswall said, "When a man is hungry and thinks he hasn't got any other choice, he'll do most anything, I imagine."

Andrews ran a hand along Shep's back and scratched behind the big dog's ears. "I imagine you're right."

They found Fort Quitman abandoned except for a lone watchman. He begged them to linger for another day or two beyond the single night they passed among the otherwise vacant buildings of the compound, but they pressed on, telling him their errand urged them. By the time they were a day's ride past there, the country had broadened out, on the American side of the river, at least. The mountains retreated to the north and east, and the land around the river was unremittingly flat and soggy. It sucked at the horses' hooves with every step, and there was no shelter from the cold wind that drove the rain into their faces and forced it into gaps in their slickers. The last leg of the journey into Ysleta was tedious: the level, monotonous river plain giving way now and then to soaked sand hills bounded on the horizon by hollows, ravines, and gorges filling and releasing the rainwater anywhere it could go onto the prairie floor.

On their left, the Rio Grande, less than a hundred yards from the trail into Ysleta, flowed along as it had forever: a thin sheet of muddy water, less than fifty yards wide, and less than six feet in its deepest channel. Or so it had been, according to the ranch hands they encountered hereabout. If this rain held up, the river would doubtless get deeper and wider. They saw no need to ride into the channel to test the theory.

When they reached irrigated farmlands spreading on both sides of the river around the Mexican village of San Agustín, they knew they were nearing their destination. Soon, in the last of the gray light of day, they saw in the rapidly descending darkness the blurred lights of Ysleta.

But the gates of the old pueblo where the Ranger station was housed were already barred for the night. The old Tigua man crouched in the watchman's hut either could not speak English or didn't want to be bothered by two bedraggled travelers, coming to him after dark. Tired, wet, and chafing at every place where skin passed over skin, Andrews and Wiswall reined their sagging mounts away from the gate and splashed through the puddles toward the village called El Paso del Norte.

To the partners' relief, they happened upon a small hostelry before going too far, and there was a livery stable next door. Though neither building resembled anything new or luxurious, to the travelers it may as well have been Buckingham Palace.

"You boys are about the sorriest sight I seen in a month," the jovial liveryman said as he came outside, raising his coal-oil lantern for a better look as the two dismounted. "You been riding these hosses, or toting them?"

"Friend, you don't have time to listen to our story," Andrews said, managing a weary smile. "Do you have room for our horses?"

"Reckon they can share a stall?"

"They've shared poorer accommodations."

"Well, all right, then. Pull them saddles off and bring 'em inside. I think I got some oats left." He turned away and unlatched the main door of the stable as Andrews and Wiswall tugged loose the latigos holding the cinches.

Inside, they helped the liveryman rub down the horses. Their damp coats steamed in the warm stable, and they were so worn out that the men nearly had to shove them the few steps into the low-walled stall they would share for the night.

"Four bits for each animal," the liveryman said, then held out his hand as Andrews counted the coins into his palm.

"Would you happen to know if the establishment next door will let us keep our dog with us?" Wiswall said.

"Don't rightly know, but you're welcome to leave him here with me. He can sleep on that pile of empty sacks over in that corner yonder, and I got a soup bone or two I can give him."

"We'd be much obliged," Andrews said. "What would that run us?"

"No charge," the liveryman said. "He don't look like he'd be much trouble."

"I don't imagine he will," Wiswall said. Leaning over and looking Shep in the eye, he said, "Go lie down over there, boy." He pointed at the wrinkled pile of burlap in the corner and walked a few paces toward it before turning back toward the dog. "Come on, Shep. Lie down. Over here."

The dog paced slowly in the direction Wiswall had indicated, with a backward glance or two. He sniffed the sacks, looked back at his masters one more time, then lay down with a heavy sigh.

"Well, if that don't beat all!" the liveryman said, grinning. "How long did it take you to train him to do that?"

"He just seems to understand," Andrews said, looking at Shep. "You'll stay, won't you, boy?" he said, addressing the dog.

Shep gave his tail a weary wag, then another.

The liveryman let out a cackle. "I do declare he sure enough savvies English! Well, I'll look after him for you, and glad to do it. He'll be right there in the morning when you come, like enough."

CHAPTER FOUR

In the morning, feeling considerably more like human beings after hot baths and a good night's sleep, Andrews and Wiswall came downstairs and approached the sleepy-looking clerk at the shabby bar of the establishment, which also served as the front desk of the hostelry.

"Where might a man get breakfast nearby?" Andrews asked.

The clerk had a neck like a buzzard's. He yawned noisily as he considered the question. "Closest chop house is back toward the pueblo," he said, pointing. "But if you can wait a bit, I'll fix you some eggs, if we've got any."

Noticing the dark crescents beneath the fellow's fingernails, Andrews said, "Back toward the pueblo, you said?"

The man nodded, scratching his head.

"One more question," said Wiswall. "Do you have a secure room here where we can lock up our valuables while we go into town?"

"Gents, I believe I can help you with that," came a booming voice from behind them.

Looking past Andrews and Wiswall, the sallow clerk straightened up his posture noticeably. "I was just about to fix them some breakfast, Mr. Corcoran," he said.

"Never mind that, Simpkins." A large man with florid complexion and a black, handlebar mustache came toward them from the front door. "Would our strong box be secure enough for you?" he said in a soft Irish brogue, gesturing toward a small office visible through a doorway behind the bar where the clerk sat.

The partners followed Corcoran into the room and saw a large safe that stood chest-height. Shielding the dial from them, Corcoran spun it back and forth a few times and turned the large steel handle. He grunted as he tugged open the steel door. He turned to look at them. "Would this be enough room for your goods, gentlemen?"

Andrews nodded. "I believe so, yes. And would we be able to retrieve them, say, later this afternoon?"

"Certainly. I'll write you a receipt for your belongings, and I'll be close by, all day; Simpkins will know where to find me. Come whenever you like."

Andrews and Wiswall went back to their room and retrieved the two canvas bags containing their rifles and extra ammunition.

Corcoran gave a careful, appraising gaze at the bags. "I believe I see the muzzle of a Sharps sticking out of the top of that bag, don't I? And from the sound and the heft, I'd say that's not the only weapon you fellows brought with you. May I?"

Wiswall nodded, and Corcoran, a pad and pencil in hand, peered into first one bag, then the other, jotting down a description of the contents. When he finished and stepped back, Wiswall swung the heavy door shut, turned the handle, and spun the dial.

"We've had a long ride through a good deal of uncertain country," Andrews said. "We thought it best to be well armed."

"I would say so," Corcoran said, nodding. "Especially these days."

"I presume you're talking about Victorio," Wiswall said.

"The same." Corcoran tore off the sheet on which he had written. "Will this do?"

Andrews studied the receipt for a moment and then nodded. He handed the paper back to Corcoran, who signed with a flourish at the bottom, then passed it back to Andrews, who affixed his customary, small and tidy signature. He folded the paper and tucked it in the breast pocket of his shirt.

"Things will be a good deal more settled, I expect, once the army re-garrisons Fort Quitman, down the river a ways," the innkeeper said.

"We rode past there on our way here," Wiswall said. "Completely deserted, except for a watchman named John Ford who claimed he used to be a Texas Ranger."

Corcoran nodded. "The last Buffalo Soldiers rode out of there near three years ago this month. But with Victorio on the loose, I hear they've taken a notion to send a detachment back in, maybe from over Fort Davis way."

"Victorio seems to be on the minds of a good number of folks," Andrews said.

"Damned well ought to be. We've got to get this country cleaned up," Corcoran said. "There's talk of the railroad coming through here, pretty soon. Likely, we'll have new folks coming to town, building houses, buying livestock … won't do to have a filthy, marauding savage running loose through the countryside."

"I reckon not," Wiswall said after a lengthy pause.

"We'll be going now," Andrews said, "but we'll be back this afternoon. I imagine we'll want our room for another night, at least."

"Make yourselves at home, gents," Corcoran boomed, clapping them both on the shoulder. "Always have rooms for paying guests."

When they walked in the front door of the livery, Shep bounded up from his corner to meet them, wagging his tail vigorously.

"Boys, I don't know how you done it, but that dog's smarter than some people I met. Stayed right there on them bags, like you told him, and never a peep out of him all night," the liveryman said.

They asked the liveryman if he knew of anyone with pack burros to sell. Not to their surprise, given their luck thus far, he didn't. They paid fifty cents apiece to hire two fresh horses for the day, and the liveryman selected two mounts from among those stabled inside.

"We'll ride into El Paso and look around a bit, then be back later today," Wiswall said, pulling his saddle off the rail.

"Suit yourselves, boys," the liveryman said. "Leave your dog here with me, if you've a notion."

"No, he'll come with us," Wiswall said.

For the first morning in many, the sky showed patches of blue between the dirty white clouds. The air was cool but with little wind, and their horses were fresh. Andrews and Wiswall set them at a brisk trot toward El Paso del Norte, and Shep paced them easily, loping in his customary position in the van.

The road was level, if pocked with puddles, and they came to the town in a little over an hour. The ride made them remember their hunger, and they ducked into an eatery that didn't look entirely unpromising. For a quarter-dollar each, they filled up on fried steak, flapjacks, and coffee, saving scraps for Shep, waiting patiently outside the doorway.

Andrews and Wiswall walked across the street toward a large, new-looking guest house called the Central Hotel.

"Looks like everybody in town could stay here," Wiswall said with a chuckle. "Can't be more than seven or eight hundred souls here, altogether."

"Well, you heard our innkeeper; they've got big plans."

They noted the presence of a schoolhouse near the edge of the small business district, a ramshackle sheriff's office, and a bawdy house. An adobe structure called the Pony Saloon featured a stack of empty beer barrels out front. Ox wains, likely waiting for loads of goods to be transported up the old Camino Real to Santa Fe and points north, sat beneath the bare branches of the gray oaks lining the street. They sauntered past the Casa Grande Dry Goods Store and Mundy Brothers, a meat market and wholesaler. Noticing a sign that read, "Lightbody & James / Clothing, Boots, Shoes, Hats," Andrews and Wiswall decided it was time to improve their apparel from the ragged, saddle- and weather-worn duds they'd had on all across Texas.

"Seems as though no one is going to sell us any burros," Andrews remarked as they stepped through the entry of the clothing store. "We might as well spend a little of our money on some better clothes."

"Lead on, partner," Wiswall said, "I'm close behind."

When they had secured for themselves sturdy trousers, two shirts each, good woolen coats, and crisp, brimmed hats, they decided that new boots were also in order. "What's the use of new clothes if your boots look like something Shep has been chewing on?" Wiswall said.

"I couldn't agree more," Andrews said.

As the clerk toted up their purchases and they made payment, Andrews inquired the direction to Fort Bliss.

"Four miles as the crow flies, northeast of town," the clerk said, pointing.

They tied their parcels to their saddles and aimed toward the army post.

CHAPTER FIVE

-

The northeast route they were advised to take led over to a muddy track named Main Street and past a dozen structures of various sizes, some of adobe, some wood framed. The lane was lined with hitching-rails, saddled horses tied to them; covered wagons of various kinds parked parallel.

"Seems they've got nearly as many saloons as people in this town," Andrews remarked.

"More cathouses than churches, for sure."

"They pay better, most likely."

They slowed their ride long enough to peek inside one of the grog parlors. A large, open room held a bar, several tables and chairs, and a billiards table. Even at this early hour, rowdy patrons filled the place. Stairs ascended the back wall, leading to whatever enterprise—pleasure salon or gambling den—was housed on the second floor.

Just as they were turning to leave, a large, pot-bellied man staggered through the open doorway. Andrews and Wiswall ducked aside to let him pass, but Shep happened to be looking the other way, watching a cat slinking by on the other side of the street. The man stumbled over Shep, barely maintaining his already-impaired balance.

"Get outta my way, you damn mutt!" he said. He aimed a kick at Shep's ribs, and the dog yelped as he leaped aside.

Before Andrews could register what had happened, Wiswall had strode to the much larger man and grabbed two handfuls of his shirt front. "Keep away from my dog, you drunken bastard." He shoved the man roughly, and the fellow fell on his back in the muddy street. He blinked for a moment, and then struggled to his feet, grunting and swearing in a slurred voice. When he stood up, he was a good half-head taller than Wiswall, who stood in front of him, fists balled up at his sides.

By now a few men had strolled to the doorway of the saloon to watch the ruckus. Andrews moved a little closer to Wiswall, keeping one eye on his partner and the other on the observers.

"You son of a bitch, I'll whip you good," the drunk said, pushing his chest toward Wiswall.

"You'll be a damned sight better off trying to whip me than if you kick my dog again," Wiswall said in an even voice.

The drunk stared at Wiswall for a few seconds, and then he peered groggily at the knot of onlookers. He made an exasperated noise and stomped away, his backside covered with mud from the nape of his neck to the heels of his boots.

A few of the men behind Andrews snickered as they turned and went back inside.

Andrews went over to Wiswall and handed him his hat, which had fallen off when Wiswall shoved the man. "Well, I reckon we'd best be on our way to Fort Bliss," he said.

Wiswall grabbed his hat and jammed it onto his head. He stared at the retreating drunk for a couple of seconds, and then turned toward his horse. "Come on, Shep," he said.

<<line space>>

Just before noon, Andrews and Wiswall hauled up in front of the headquarters of the commander of Fort Bliss. They looped their reins over the hitching rail in front of the handsome, two-story frame building with a broad porch.

"Stay here, Shep," Andrews said, pointing to a spot on the porch next to the front door. The dog settled himself against the wall and laid his head on his front paws. The travelers went inside.

After explaining their errand to the satisfaction of the sergeant major in the anteroom, they were ushered into the office of Major N. W. Osbourne.

"Have a seat, gentlemen," Osbourne said after the introductions were concluded. Settling himself back behind his desk, he said, "How may I be of assistance?"

"Major, we have made a long and, so far, fruitless journey through nearly the whole of Texas, with the purpose of procuring a stock of burros to take back with us to the mining country in Ouray County, Colorado, where we come from,"

Andrews said. "But we have lately had to admit to ourselves that we are whipped, and now our only aim is to go home by the most direct route and as soon as possible. We are aware of the dangers of such a journey, however."

"Victorio," the major said.

Andrews nodded. "Certainly. And so, Major, our first interest is to know whether, within any reasonable time, you expect to dispatch a patrol or some other movement toward the north and east, especially in the vicinity of the valleys of the Pecos River? If you do, we would earnestly request to accompany them, as far as their orders take them, in order to safely come that much closer to our destination in southern Colorado."

Osbourne had begun shaking his head, even before Andrews finished his request. "I am sorry, Mr. Andrews, but I will not be able to help you in this matter. Not in the dead of winter—one of the wettest and windiest we have had for some years, I might add. To send men out at such a time, absent the direst need, would not be the wisest use of our forces. And besides all that, we have only infantry here—no cavalry."

Andrews thought this over for a few seconds. "Very well, Major; we understand your position. So, then, to our second question: We find it advisable to equip ourselves with a wagon or similar conveyance that might be pulled by a small team. Is it possible that your quartermaster might have such a piece of equipment, perhaps used, that we could purchase?"

Osbourne scratched his chin for a moment. "Now, there, I might be able to help you. Sergeant Foster, could you come in here, please?"

The sergeant-major stepped into the doorway. "Sir?"

"Take these men to Lieutenant Kinzie, and ask him to give them any aid in his power, according to their request."

"Yes, sir."

"I believe that we have something that might be just right for your needs," the major said. "Sergeant Foster will show you the way. I wish you good luck and Godspeed, gentlemen, though I would be remiss if I didn't advise you to winter with us here in El Paso or Ysleta and make your journey in better weather and on safer roads."

"Thank you, Major," Andrews said, standing and shaking the commander's hand, "but we have taken it in mind to go home, and we mean to make the attempt. We are grateful for your time."

"Yes, indeed," Osbourne said, shaking Wiswall's hand.

"This way, gentlemen," the sergeant-major said, gesturing toward the front door.

With Shep tagging along at their heels, the three men strode across the wide parade ground. As they went, Andrews asked their guide if he had any knowledge of the old Butterfield Stage road that led east, past the Hueco Tanks, toward the Pecos River.

"Well, no one goes that way much these days," he said. "It's not judged safe unless you're with an armed convoy."

"Granted, but what about the terrain?" Andrews said. "What kind of rig would a man need to have to manage the trip to the Pecos, going that way?"

"That there is some pretty rough country," the sergeant-major said. "You'd need some good, sturdy stock, I reckon. The terrain is likely why the Butterfield stopped traveling that way, going on twenty-two years ago, near-about."

"It sounds to me as though we had better trade our ponies for a couple of stout draft horses," Wiswall said.

"And the harness for them," Andrews said, nodding.

They arrived at the quartermaster's post. Sergeant Foster made introductions, gave Shep a scratch behind the ears, and left them. Lieutenant Kinzie listened carefully to their intentions and their planned route.

"Gentlemen, how much are you willing to spend on your conveyance?"

They told him that they could hardly afford anything large enough to require a four-animal team—or the animals to draw it, for that matter.

"Well …" The quartermaster tapped a finger on his temple as he thought. "I do have one of the Coolidge ambulances in surplus. I don't believe it has been too hard-used. Would you like to come over to the shed and take a look at it?"

The two-wheeled Coolidge was built to accommodate two men on stretchers, lying side by side. It also had a fair amount of shelf space above the bed, it was roofed and curtained against the elements, and best of all, it could be handily drawn by two horses. The lieutenant warned them that this particular model had acquired the unaffectionate nickname "The Avalanche" because of the sometimes bone-jarring ride it delivered, running as it did on only two wheels and lacking much in the way of springs or other suspension. But as a light conveyance that offered a place for sleeping other than the cold ground, Andrews and Wiswall concluded that the Coolidge fit their bill.

"I'll wager we could find a small, cast-iron heating stove that we could rig up inside," Andrews said, pointing here and there at the ambulance's interior. "And those look like iron-hubbed wheels to me."

"If I'm not mistaken, we have some extra harness we can let you have at no cost," Lieutanant Kinzie said. "That will save you some money. And yes, this ambulance has an iron running gear and wheel hubs. You'll need that if you take the route you intend."

By the time they had completed negotiations, the quartermaster made them a price just over $100; Andrews later told Wiswall he calculated that was less than half the price of a new ambulance.

"We don't have any surplus horses," Kinzie told them as he wrote out a bill of sale. "But if I were you fellows, I would ride over to Ysleta. There's a livery right next to a hotel run by an Irishman, and the owner is about as good a judge of horseflesh as anybody I know in these parts. If anyone hereabout has got good pulling stock, he'll know about it."

Andrews and Wiswall realized the lieutenant was directing them back to the livery where they had started earlier that day. "We know the place and the man," Andrews said. "We'll inquire of him, as you suggest."

"Too bad he doesn't traffic in armed guards," Wiswall said, scuffing the toe of his boot on the rough floor planking. "The major informed us that the army wasn't heading our way any time soon."

"Meaning no offense, but you ought to attend carefully to the major's advice," Lieutenant Kinzie said. "Victorio is about as wily as they come. I'm plenty satisfied to sit out the winter here at the fort, and not ashamed to say it."

"I expect you're right about all of that," Andrews said. "But we mean to go home, and we are still holding out hope of locating some burros we can sell, along the way."

"Well, if you're dead-set, you ought to inquire at the Ranger station, back in Ysleta," Kinzie said. "Civilian escort is one of their usual missions, though I can't say I'd bet heavily on Baylor sending men with you, any more than Major Osbourne did."

"It now seems that we have at least two errands waiting for us back in Ysleta," Wiswall said. "I reckon we'd best be on our way while there's plenty of daylight left."

"We will come back by tomorrow to retrieve the ambulance, once we've secured a team." Andrews said.

The quartermaster nodded. "I'll have your rig greased and waiting for you."

CHAPTER SIX

-

The old Indian who had denied them entry the night before was nowhere in sight when Andrews and Wiswall arrived at the entry to the post housing Company C in the Frontier Battalion, Texas Rangers. The gates of the old pueblo stood wide open, and men and horses passed through in both directions, all seemingly intent upon some errand or other.

The Rangers of Company C resided in what appeared to be a warehouse, or block-house of sorts. According to the signage, painted slapdash on a whitewashed board, part of the low, flat-roofed structure housed Chilvers and Keirle Company, Outfitters. The other part, perhaps one-third of the building, was the Rangers' sleeping quarters, mess, and relaxation area. They saw, scattered around the pueblo premises, stables, other small structures and adobe dwellings, and one large, well-appointed adobe house fronted by a wide porch.

Unable to catch anyone's attention long enough to obtain guidance as to Lieutenant Baylor's whereabouts, the travelers made for the block-house, which seemed to be the focus of a good deal of activity. With Shep padding along at their heels, they entered a large, well-lit room.

They noticed a man molding bullets near a fireplace on the far wall. Others milled about or sat in threes and fours at plank tables, some cleaning guns or mending tack, and others playing monte or faro with creased cards. One corner of the room held a pile of saddles and harnesses.

"Excuse me, friend, but can you direct me toward Lieutenant Baylor?" Wiswall said to a man sitting by himself, studying a soiled newspaper. He looked up at Wiswall for a moment, then at Andrews. Finally his eyes fell upon Shep, who wagged his tail slowly. One corner of the man's heavy mustache lifted slightly, and he aimed a forefinger over Wiswall's shoulder, through the doorway by which they had just entered. "This time of day, he's generally setting on the porch of his house, yonder." Wiswall touched his hat brim, and they went in the direction indicated. They walked across the muddy yard of the pueblo toward the house, and true to the man's word, they saw a tall, strong figure of a man seated on the porch of the house, draped in a loose-limbed posture on a low bench that somewhat resembled a church pew.

Lieutenant George Wythe Baylor had a narrow, intelligent face, clear blue eyes, and a demeanor of quick and quiet interest in whatever was going on around him. He now focused that interest on Andrews and Wiswall as they approached. "Evening, gentlemen. That is a fine-looking dog you've got with you, there."

"Thank you, sir. I presume you to be Lieutenant Baylor?" Andrews said.

"Guilty as charged," Baylor said with a smile. "And to whom do I have the honor of speaking?" Andrews introduced himself and Wiswall to Baylor, and the three men shook hands all around.

Andrews told the Ranger commander what they had on their minds. Baylor gazed off into the distance as he listened, and for a good, long while after Andrews had finished his request, he continued in what looked like a thoughtful silence.

"No, fellows, I will not be able to send men with you," he said, finally. "And I will also urge you to reconsider your travel plans."

"Thank you, Lieutenant," Andrews said, "and I assure you that you are not the first to question the wisdom of our intentions, with good reason, in all likelihood. But we are firm in our purpose. We have taken care of ourselves thus far on this long journey, and we believe we can see ourselves home on our own, if we have to."

Baylor nodded slowly. "Well, I can't fault your resolve, at least. But may I at least counsel you, as one who has made a careful study of the Mescalero people and their habits and who also knows a little about traveling through this country?"

The lieutenant told Andrews and Wiswall that, if they were determined to go to the upper Pecos country, they should start back the way they had come, but veer sooner to the east, taking the overland stage route to Fort Davis, in the Big Bend country. From there, he told them, they might work their way along Toyah Creek and come to the Pecos drainage by a much safer route.

"That sounds like a lot of backtracking to me, Lieutenant," Andrews said when Baylor had finished. "The way straight to the east would save us a good deal of time."

"What you may save in time, friend, you risk in danger. Let me tell you some of what I have learned in these last months, while I have been pursuing Victorio and his raiders …"

As Baylor talked about Victorio and his renegade band, men were steadily passing to and fro across the pueblo yard. Most of those who passed anywhere near Baylor's front porch made enough of a detour to stoop down and scratch Shep's head or rub along his neck. Before long, even Lieutenant Baylor started to notice the dog's spontaneous popularity with his Rangers.

"Your dog has winning ways, I judge," he said, grinning. "How long have you had him?"

"We picked him up back in the late summer, on our way down into Texas from Colorado," Wiswall said. He patted a hand along Shep's ribs. "He's made a pretty good companion, all told."

"He is as well-mannered as any dog in my experience," Baylor said.

"Yes, he behaves himself," Andrews said. "We three seem to understand each other pretty well."

"Where did you find him?"

"Fort Sill, in the Indian Territory," Wiswall said. "Some soldiers there … had him. We got him from them."

Andrews recognized the hard, flat line of his partner's voice as he recollected the day they'd first seen Shep. He cleared his throat. "Well, Lieutenant, I expect we've taken up enough of your time. We've got some business over at the livery that we need to conclude, so I guess we'll be taking our leave."

"Certainly, gentlemen, certainly. But may I at least invite you to take a meal with me before you strike out on the trail?"

"I'm not in the habit of refusing good food that is freely offered," Andrews said with a wry smile.

"Very well! Why don't you take the day tomorrow to provision yourselves, and then come back here about this same time of the evening? My wife and daughters would enjoy getting to know your dog, there, and I'd relish the opportunity to tuck some good, home-cooked food into you before you head back out into the wilderness."

"We'd be honored, Lieutenant," Andrews said as Wiswall nodded eagerly.

"That's settled, then. I'll look for you tomorrow evening. And my sergeant, Jim Gillett, will be there, too. You'll like him."

<<line break>>

The next morning, the livery stable owner proved as good as Lieutenant Kinzie's assessment. He led them to a corral behind his barn and pointed out two heavy-limbed, stocky geldings, one a solid sorrel and the other a bay with a white off forefoot and a blaze down his face. "I just got them from a fellow over Mesilla way. He'll take a hundred for the pair. I guarantee you they're in good shape—at least, I'm pretty sure they are, as much oats and hay as I've put through 'em."

"That certainly seems a fair price," Wiswall said.

"You won't do no better anywhere around here, I promise you," the liveryman said. "These here hosses can pull anything you got, up any hill you're likely to see."

"What can you give us for the ponies we rode in on?" Andrews said.

The liveryman scratched his head. "Well, them hosses are pretty wore out. But they still look sound, and with a little rest and some oats … I expect I could go twenty-five each."

After Andrews had patted down both horses, feeling their legs and walking around them a couple of times each, they shook hands with the liveryman. Andrews gave him the trade difference in cash, and they agreed on a time later that morning when they would pick up their new team and take it to the fort to retrieve the ambulance.

They found the ambulance just as Kinzie had promised, and with the team hitched up, it appeared that they would have the means to make the trip to the upper Pecos in at least some measure of comfort. The partners spent the rest of the afternoon securing enough beans, sowbelly, and coffee to carry them to Pope's Crossing on the Pecos and, with luck, a little beyond. Almost as an afterthought, they struck a deal with the liveryman for a saddle horse, reasoning that it might be well for one of them to serve as a kind of outrider on their two-man expedition.

The clouds were starting to close in again as evening began to draw down. The partners even felt a drop or two of rain as they walked across the yard of the pueblo toward the Baylor house, fronted by the broad veranda where they had met the post commander the day before.

Andrews and Wiswall, with Shep following at their side, walked up the steps to the wide porch, and Baylor stood smiling at the front door. "This fellow can come on in with you," he said, nodding toward Shep. "He is one of our guests of honor, after all."

The living room was warm and neatly carpeted. As they entered, a young man rose from his seat on a small sofa near a thriving fire in the brick fireplace. "Gentlemen, meet Sergeant Gillett," Baylor said. "Sergeant, these are Andrews and Wiswall, from up Colorado way, and this is Shep, their four-footed partner."

The sergeant shook hands with the two and leaned down to pat Shep on the head. About then, a middle-aged woman and two girls in their early teens entered simultaneously. Baylor presented his wife and his two daughters. The girls gave pretty curtsies and immediately dropped to their knees on either side of Shep, who welcomed their joyful patter and petting with some vigorous tail-wagging.

Later, discussing the very pleasant evening, Andrews and Wiswall would agree that the sofas, chairs, table, and well-filled bookcases in the Baylor home would not have been an embarrassment to any in New York or Baltimore. A pistol, loaded and capped, lay on the mantelpiece, and through the glass windows of a second bookcase Wiswall spotted a small collection of Indian knives. Mrs. Baylor went into the kitchen and returned with iced water, glasses, and a bottle of excellent claret, a refreshment most welcomed by the mining engineers.

Sergeant Gillett proved an interesting companion. To Andrews and Wiswall's eye, he had an air of distinction about him, a quiet dignity demanding respect. Although there was nothing about him suggesting toughness or ruggedness, there was certainly nothing weak in his demeanor. What impressed them the most was how Gillett's weathered face, though still youthful, held cool, watchful eyes. As the pre-dinner conversation progressed, they learned about his last five years with the Texas Rangers, and especially about his experiences during the recent Red River Wars with the Kiowa, Comanche, and Lipan Apache.

When the small party was called into the dining room a few minutes later, Andrews and Wiswall were pleased to note the care evident in the place settings and the arrangement of the surroundings. A quiet Mexican woman was placing the last pitcher of water on the table when they came in, and the travelers watched as Baylor held his wife's chair while she took her seat. They noted, too, a certain solicitousness in Gillett as he performed the same duty for Baylor's older daughter.

They ate, politely chattering about any subject that came to mind: the unusual amounts of wind and rain for West Texas thus far in the winter; the possibility of an economic boom for El Paso now that three railroad companies were in the planning stages of putting lines through the area; the principal problems facing Texas and the nation; the ineptitude and graft presently rampant in Washington, DC. Wiswall made their standard inquiry after the availability of burros for purchase and received the same reply that had dogged them since arriving in Texas. They weren't surprised, as their dependable liveryman had already assured them that no one around had sufficient animals to satisfy their request.

"Well, fellows, you need to eat your fill," Baylor said, passing the bowl of roasted vegetables back to Wiswall. "I don't imagine you'll have similar victuals on the trail."

"Lieutenant, beans and bacon don't make much show alongside a baked Virginia ham, homemade apple butter, hot biscuits, and everything else I see here," Andrews said, raising smiles from the others. "And, ma'am," he said, looking at Mrs. Baylor, "I can't provide sufficient superlatives for the way everything tastes."

"What the Harvard man is saying," Wiswall said as he busily forked vegetables onto his plate, "is that this is the best meal we've sat down to since … well, I don't know when."

Everyone laughed. "Mr. Wiswall, I thank you," Mrs. Baylor said, "though we all know that hunger is the best sauce. I expect it has been a while since you had any sort of home-cooked food."

"Yes, ma'am. But I'll carry the memory of this meal all the way back to Ouray County, I can promise you. I'd like to send my fiancée down here to take some cooking lessons."

"Well, I shouldn't put it to her that way, if I were you," Mrs. Baylor said, "but I would be delighted by her company, I'm sure."

Shep was enjoying himself, too. Now and again, Andrews or Wiswall would feel the dog slide back and forth against their legs, beneath the table, as first one, then another would drop tidbits for him. No one seemed to mind at all.

After supper, with the women clearing the table and retiring to the kitchen to wash the dishes, Baylor produced pipes, tobacco, and a leather flask of El Paso port, a special fortified dark wine of rich aroma and sharp taste from the grapes grown along the banks of the Rio Grande. He motioned the three men to the large, comfortable chairs positioned before the fireplace.

As Andrews, Wiswall, and Gillett sat and stretched their legs, Baylor lit his pipe. He took a deep pull and let the blue smoke out slowly. Looking first at Wiswall, then at Andrews, he said, "I must tell you straight from the shoulder; you won't make it if you head up towards the Pecos by yourselves, especially in this cold and wet weather. You'll need at least ten days for the 150-mile journey, with Victorio and his band potentially behind every rock or waiting in ambush up ahead."

Shep was curled in front of the fire, and his hindquarters lay near Baylor's feet. The lieutenant gently rubbed the dog with the toe of his boot. "As recently as a month and a half ago, around the end of November, a party of Mescalero Apaches left the reservation after killing an ox and fifteen head of sheep. They packed the meat and headed south on six horses they had just stolen. Inasmuch as the meat is well in excess of their present needs, I think it likely that this is only a foraging party for a much larger force planning to take the field, perhaps in the very area you plan to travel through.

"In our nearby Sacramento Mountains, two miners, Fred Asbecks and William Mann, were chased out during the first week of December. We got word by a telegram from the Adjutant General on the tenth of December that Victorio and his war party were the culprits. Mann knows Victorio well and saw him in person.

"Just a week ago, in the general area you plan to travel through the San Mateo Mountains, there have been skirmishes with Victorio, and he has held his own, maneuvering easily through country so rough that it broke down our US Cavalry men and horses in just a few days of scouting.

"Not long ago, some of Victorio's people jumped a mail coach about sunrise near Fort Cummings, a six-company post about ninety or a hundred miles northwest, up Deming way. They killed every mortal on the coach; their blood soaked the mail sacks."

The fire popped as a log settled in a cloud of sparks. Baylor looked into the flames for a few seconds, then said, "I tell you gentlemen all this to make you aware of where you are and who you're dealing with, in hopes that I can persuade you against your plan and so that you can retain your scalps."

For a time, there was no sound except the soft popping of the fire and the muted talk of the women in the kitchen. "Lieutenant, we thank you for this information and the sincere concern that motivates it," Andrews said, finally. "But we are well armed and adequately provisioned—not to mention abundantly forewarned. I think—and I believe I can speak for Mr. Wiswall, also—we mean to go ahead."

CHAPTER SEVEN

-

Before sunrise the next morning, Andrews and Wiswall had settled their accounts with Corcoran, retrieved their weaponry from his safe, and were at the livery harnessing their new team and saddling their other horse. They lingered in Ysleta only long enough to procure a used but serviceable small wood stove and to rig it securely on the inside of the ambulance. And then, a little before noon on Sunday, with the lanky Andrews astride the saddle horse and the stocky Wiswall driving the two-wheeled ambulance, they set out to the east for the Pecos River along the abandoned stagecoach trail that had once been the Butterfield Overland Mail route. Shep, of course, trotted along in front. The two men remarked to each other that, after nineteen years of neglect, the trail was in surprisingly good shape. The coach and wagon tracks were easily visible.

They hoped to come without incident to the old Hueco Tanks station, some thirty miles east of El Paso. With fresh horses in harness and if the terrain didn't become too demanding too soon, they hoped that they might reach the station before dark of the second day of travel.

"Well, what do you plan to say to old Victorio, when we meet up with him on the road?" Andrews asked as the Coolidge ambulance jounced along beside him on the rutted trail.

"I will give him the time of day," Wiswall said, "and inquire after the health of his family. We'll discuss the weather, and I expect we'll both have the same opinion of it. And then, no doubt, we'll part company as great friends and go our separate ways."

Andrews gave a low chuckle. "I didn't think you knew so much of the Apache lingo as all that."

"My Apache is about as good as your Spanish," Wiswall quipped.

"Then we're both in trouble, I reckon."

Wiswall laughed.

On that first day the weather, for once, did them a service; though the sky was gray and the wind blustery, they at least were able to travel dry and on a track that didn't threaten to mire the ambulance to the axles. By late afternoon, the miniature caravan had made its way past the last of the barren hills east of El Paso and had crawled onto the broad, open desert of the Hueco Bolson that separated the Franklin Mountains to the west from the Diablo Plateau, to the east. As far as they could see in any direction, the low scrub of the northern Chihuahua desert stretched away toward the horizon. In the dingy, winter light, the creosote, ocotillo, and three-awn grass surrounded them like a grayish-silver sea.

As the sky darkened and the temperature dropped, Andrews and Wiswall began surveying the terrain for a secluded spot to camp. They calculated they had covered almost half of the distance to the Hueco Tanks since leaving Ysleta, just before noon. But now a slight drizzle had started up, guaranteeing a cold, uncomfortable night. Neither man was interested in spending it on the open trail.

Soon enough, they spotted an arroyo with a few low, sheltering hackberry trees growing along its edges. They pulled off the trail and worked their way down into the little ravine. The bottom was muddy from the recent rains, but it offered some shelter from the wind and at least partial concealment from any unfriendly eyes that might pass in the night.

As Andrews placed hobbles on the three horses, Wiswall made a small fire in the ambulance's tiny built-in stove to heat a supper of bacon, beans, and three-day-old bread. The horses nosed along the ground, cropping such goosefoot and grama grass as they could find on the lower sides of the arroyo.

After supper, Andrews and Wiswall stretched their legs and emptied their bladders and bowels as Shep ranged here and there around the campsite. Presently Wiswall whistled and the dog came trotting back. The three climbed into the ambulance for a night's sleep.

"Well, the Coolidge lived up to its nickname, all right," Wiswall said as the two men settled onto their cots. "Like to have drove my tailbone up through my gizzard, a couple of times. But for all that, this surely beats sleeping on the ground."

Andrews made a few small grunts as he arranged his long legs on the cot. "And tomorrow I'll take my turn in the driver's seat; you can ride the pony."

Shep curled at their feet, just inside the opening of the cart.

"What do you say, Shep?" Andrews said. "Will this little wagon do for our home on the trail?"

Hearing his name, the dog lifted his head and looked at Andrews, then at Wiswall. He laid his muzzle back on his paws and closed his eyes.

"I believe you can mark that as a 'yea' vote," Wiswall said.

"I expect so."

Silence fell, broken only by the occasional click of a horseshoe against a rock.

The next morning, they woke to the all-too-familiar patter of rain on the canvas cover of the ambulance.

"I knew the balmy weather was too good to last," Wiswall said as he yawned and stretched. "Go on, Shep; get up off my feet. We're going to travel damp today; might as well get used to it."

Shep raised himself up and, looking more than a little reluctant, hopped down onto the ground. Andrews and Wiswall rolled up their blankets and stowed them in the shelves above the cots. Wiswall shrugged into his slicker and crawled outside to remove the hobbles from the horses and bring the team to harness.

Andrews found a live coal in the little stove and carefully fed it some dry twigs he found under a tangled windfall. Before too long, the water in the coffee pot was boiling. He took the pot off the stove and let it cool for a bit, then he dropped in a scoop or two of coffee and poured in a little cold water to settle the grounds. By the time Wiswall had the team hitched and the pony saddled, Andrews was able to hand him a steaming tin cup.

"Time we've gone about five miles, I'll need another one of these," Wiswall said as he took his first sip.

"How far do you calculate we are from Hueco Tanks?" Andrews said, handing Wiswall a piece of toasted bread.

"I'd say half a day, if the weather were better," Wiswall said. "But the way the air feels, this rain is liable to turn into snow any time now."

Andrews nodded. "Let's see if we can make it before dark. Maybe there's some better cover there."

"Maybe."

CHAPTER EIGHT

-

"Sergeant Gillett calculated we'd have no problem finding wood and water at every stop, especially with the rain runoffs," Wiswall remarked, riding along beside the ambulance. "With any luck, Victorio and his bunch are up in New Mexico, on the west side of the Guadalupes."

"Well, one thing's for sure," Andrews said as he jounced along on the bench of the Coolidge, "there's nothing much in this country for them to hide behind. It's about as flat as any place I've ever been."

"That's so," Wiswall said. "On the other hand, there's not much of any place for us to hide, either."

It was true that they were still in open country, and the wind drove straight across it, pushing the thickening snow flurries into their faces. Fortunately for the travelers, the old Butterfield road was easily discernable, relatively straight, and unhindered.

By midday—at least, as well as midday could be guessed with the featureless gray skies and swirling snow—Andrews and Wiswall could see the first elevation of the Hueco Mountains rising slowly in the east. Squatting just in front of that low range of mountains, the rocky outcroppings of the Hueco Tanks offered the possibility of a windbreak, and they might even find a partial roof left on the abandoned stage station.

The Hueco Tanks station had been built as a meal and change stop on the Butterfield trail. At one time it had possessed an excellent corral, cabin, storage shed, and blacksmith shop. But the trail had not been used regularly since 1859, when the Butterfield line moved south, trailing the Rio Grande well past Eagle Springs before bearing east for Fort Davis, then up to the Horsehead Crossing on the Pecos—the route Baylor had so earnestly urged on the travelers.

Now, twenty years later, Andrews and Wiswall would have to make do with crumbling stone and adobe walls, all that remained of the Butterfield Stage station after nearly two decades of nature's slow, relentless battering. They reached the stark, upthrust crags about an hour before full dark and maneuvered around the four rocky outcroppings that made up the formation until they reached the site of the old station, in a pass between the four hills and an ancient-looking reservoir—now more than half-full of rainwater and runoff.

In the fading daylight, Andrews and Wiswall could make out a few of the hundreds of mysterious paintings that decorated the rock faces and hidden grottos of the Hueco

Tanks, said to be the leavings of ancient people who hunted these plains thousands of years before. Of course, there were also more recent graffiti, scrawled by bored Buffalo Soldiers, Butterfield employees, or others with time on their hands, not only on the stone of the Tanks but also across the adobe of the abandoned station.

"My mother used to say, 'Fools' names and fools' faces always appear in public places,'" Andrews remarked as they unhitched the team and prepared their camp in the lee of one of the decrepit station walls.

"Ah, but these are historical markings, don't you know," said Wiswall. "These travelers through the sands of time have left their mark—evidence of their brief sojourn through this vale of tears."

"You might want to save some of that breath for getting the stove lit."

Shep snuffled busily about the camp, pausing at several bushes to lift a leg. After a while, he came to Wiswall's call and received a chunk of bacon, carved off the slab. He caught it in the air and chomped it eagerly, making short work of the tasty morsel.

"Looks like the snow is slowing," Andrews said a bit later as the two men sat in the shelter of the ambulance to eat their supper. "Maybe we'll make better time tomorrow."

"There's a good deal of water held in the hollows of the rocks here," Wiswall said. "We ought to refill the kegs as best we can before we set out."

In the gray of the next predawn, Wiswall harnessed the team and saddled the pony while Andrews made repeated trips to and from the nearest hollow, hueco in Spanish, for which the entire region was named. After dumping enough fresh water from their wooden pail into the kegs strapped to the outsides of the ambulance, he whistled for Shep and announced to Wiswall that it was time to set out.

Determined to press all the way through to Cornudas del Alamo by sunset, they were relieved to see that, as the morning broadened, the snow that had fallen the day before began to melt with the sun peeking through the low-scudding gray clouds. On this stretch, the Butterfield road crossed Diablo Plateau toward the Salt Flat. Their only difficulty, initially, was negotiating the winding passage up the western flanks of the Hueco Mountains in order to come out onto the plateau; in this ascent, their sturdy draft horses served them well. Once they reached the more level terrain of the plateau, they made good progress.

"What do you suppose accounts for the cruelty Victorio inflicts on his victims?" asked Wiswall as they trundled along, watching the sun climb the sky in front of them.

"Why would you ask that?" Andrews said. "Do you plan to negotiate with him, if we come upon him?"

"He just stays in my mind, that's all. I suppose I'm trying to come to terms with him as a fellow human being. And it doesn't stand to reason that a man followed by other men is cruel for no reason, unless maybe he's crazy. And it doesn't seem too likely to me that a crazy man would last long, living rough in country like this. So, there must be a method in it, somewhere."

They rode a while in thoughtful silence. Ahead of them, a jackrabbit started from its hiding place under a creosote bush, and Shep kited off after it, giving chase.

"What about those soldiers, the ones who had Shep in that pit?" Andrews said. "What purpose did that serve?"

"Stupidity and cruelty are the province of shiftless men with too much time on their hands," Wiswall said in a grim voice. "I don't fancy Victorio as a stupid man. Or an idle one."

"I didn't take too many philosophy classes back east," Andrews said after a while. "My education focused mostly on the practical matters of the engineering sphere. But I reckon that in Victorio's experience, his treatment of those he vanquishes purchases him some advantage or other. Buys him the respect of his braves, maybe."

Wiswall nodded. His face was tilted sideways and held a pondering look. "Could be. And then there's anger. He can't love the white man for what we have done to a way of life that was a going concern since long before our like first came out here."

Shep was trotting back toward them, his tongue lolling out. Apparently, the jackrabbit would live to fight another day.

"Would you have us all retrace our steps and go back east?" Andrews said. "Get back on our ships and return to England, maybe?"

"I don't calculate that program would get too far, would it?" Wiswall said.

"Quite doubtful. And don't forget; you and I base our livelihood on the assumption that folks will continue to need what comes out of the ground up Colorado way. I don't think the Utes, Apaches, or Cheyenne are going to offer much of a market for coal or lead, do you? Though one might be able to do a little business in silver, I suppose."

"True enough. But still … I can't help thinking that if I were pushed into the sort of corner Victorio and the other chiefs are in, shoved onto a reservation nothing like their home country and faced with feeding a bunch of hungry mouths … Well, I don't know what I might do."

"I doubt your philosophy would find many takers among the good townsfolk of El Paso del Norte," Andrews said. "They have a railroad to bring in and a population boom to get ready for."

"I grant that's so," Wiswall said. "None of us can turn back the clock. But I can't escape the notion that someday, there will be a reckoning for the way we've treated people like Victorio and the others. I don't know where or when, but it's coming."

"The Almighty grant that we're both pushing up daisies before that great and terrible day," Andrews said.

"Maybe less talk and more watching, then?"

"Point well taken."

By midmorning of that day, there was not a cloud in the blue sky. By noon, the dark, sharp ridges of the Cornudas Mountains rose before the small, one-carriage cavalcade as it wound through the detached hills on the outskirts of the range. As evening began to fall, they spotted the sagging, partially tumbled-down rock walls of the old stage stop. Upslope from it, some 500 feet up the side of Alamo Mountain, was the spring for which the station was named.

"Do you reckon it's worth the hike up that slope with a bucket to refill our kegs?" Wiswall said, eyeing the rocky incline. They could discern a clump of trees above them, about where they guessed the spring issued—likely cottonwoods, to account for the name the Spanish had given the place.

"Before we go all the way up there, why don't we scout among the huecos down here around us and see what they've got to offer?"

"Sound advice, I'd judge."

"That, and I've gotten plumb out of the habit of climbing hills, since we left Ouray County."

"That, too."

"On the other hand, the horses … "

They finally agreed that Wiswall would gather water for the casks from such huecos as he could locate more or less in the flat, and Andrews would ride up the slope to the spring on the pony, leading the team. Shep opted to follow the horses.

"Keep your eyes peeled," Wiswall advised as Andrews rode away.

"You do the same," Andrews called over his shoulder.

<<line break>>

After an uneventful night, Andrews and Wiswall made an early start and began crossing the desert plain in an easterly direction toward the Guadalupe Mountains and the deserted Crow Spring relay station that lay some six miles in front of them. A light drizzle had begun at about first light, but they were resolved to reach the station by nightfall, and before that if they could.

The road up the slope to the mesa where Crow Spring was situated undulated slightly as it cut through now, a profusion of cactus and yucca, now a long stretch of ocotillo interspersed with honey mesquite. In the distance, they saw the white rumps of pronghorn antelope scampering across the prairie, and closer to the old stage road they could see the round-rimmed entrances of prairie dog burrows with sentinels perched here and there, ready to sound the warning if an intruder approached. Shep tried chasing the little creatures once or twice but soon learned he could never come near them before they vanished underground with a flip of their short, wispy tails. Andrews and Wiswall judged that their laughter at his failed attempts pained the dog; Wiswall declared that he looked downright embarrassed after his second fruitless effort.

Around noon they saw the ruined walls of the station, about a hundred feet off the trail. No roof remained to the structure, but there was an acequia for leading rain runoff water into a tank in what had once been a corral, and the tank was brimming. Scattered on the ground between the roofless walls lay fragments of bottle glass and crockery, a few rusted, crushed cans, strips of decaying leather, and fragments of weather-grayed rope.

The slow rain had followed them all day, but thankfully there was little wind driving it. Huddled beneath their slickers, the partners unhitched the team, took the saddle off the pony, and led the horses to water in the corral tank. They hobbled the animals near the remaining walls of the building where they had maneuvered the ambulance, leaving them to find such grazing as they might. Shep disappeared to explore the surrounding terrain, offering an occasional yip to signify his whereabouts.

CHAPTER NINE

-

Before too long, the little stove in the Coolidge had yielded a pot of coffee, some boiled beans, and a good-sized pile of fried bacon, sliced thick off the slab. The rain had begun to slacken, but a cold north wind coursed through the broken walls of the old station, and neither man needed much encouragement to huddle inside and consume the victuals in relative comfort.

"Notice the dinner music?" Andrews asked as they sipped their coffee.

The wind swirled through the cracks in the adobe walls and around the corners, setting up a rising and falling moan.

"I've heard happier tunes," Wiswall said.

"Well, I reckon it'll do for a lullaby, maybe," Andrews said, "as long as we wake up in the morning with our scalps attached."

"Where's the dog?" Wiswall said, after a minute or two. "You heard him lately?"

"Who knows? I hope he doesn't come back carrying a rattlesnake in his mouth."

"Well, that's one good thing about this weather," Wiswall said. "I imagine it's too cold for rattlers."

"No, they've got the sense to be denned up by now," Andrews said with a little laugh. He leaned over to peek out at the sky. "Let the horses graze a bit longer. Then I'll bring them in and picket them along side of the ambulance."

Just then, they heard the sound of Shep's barking coming down the wind.

"Probably still chasing prairie dogs," Wiswall said.

"Now that he knows we can't watch."

Wiswall chuckled and nodded. "He'll come wandering in soon enough, I imagine."

The wind shook the canvas cover of the ambulance. Andrews reached into one of the cupboards and dug out a wrinkled bag of tobacco.

"Good idea," Wiswall said, fishing his stump of a clay pipe out of a shirt pocket. Andrews found a glowing ember in the stove on the end of a pencil-sized twig and set it to his pipe, drawing until he was pulling steady draughts of blue smoke. He passed the twig to Wiswall, and soon fragrant clouds drifted inside the little wagon before wisping out the front flap on the wind.

"Where do you calculate they are?" Wiswall said after a while.

"The Indians?" Andrews took a thoughtful pull and exhaled slowly. "Don't know. If they were around, you'd think we'd have seen something, as wide open as the country is hereabout."

Wiswall shrugged. "Well, if they are around, they've seen us; that's certain."

Andrews nodded. A little later, he reached over to the place where his Sharps lay along the sideboard. He thumbed open the breech and saw the cartridge, ready in the firing chamber. Carefully he closed the breech and replaced the rifle.

A thump and a jostle caused the two men to jerk upright, their hands going to their sidearms. Shep's head poked through the flap of the cover. He grinned at them from his perch on the driver's bench, his tongue lolling back and forth as he panted.

"So you've come home from the chase, have you?" Andrews said. "Lucky you didn't get yourself shot, boy. Next time, knock before you come in the house."

"Never mind him, Shep," Wiswall said, grinning as he ruffled the fur behind the dog's ears. "He's just a little keyed up." Wiswall cut a hunk of bacon from the slab and scooted it toward the shepherd, who gobbled it eagerly.

The men puffed their pipes and the wind rattled on. Shep scooted inside the cover and curled near the front of the wagon bed. Shep raised his head once, peering out the waving canvas flap in the direction from which he had come. Then he put his head back down. The men smoked; their eyelids drooped.

Shep's head jerked up again, his nostrils quivering. He sprang to his feet, barking. At that instant, Andrews and Wiswall heard whooping and shouting, accompanied by the sound of horse whinnies and hoofs striking the ground.

They grabbed their rifles and bailed out of the ambulance, Shep close on their heels. They ran to the opening in the wall and saw a small crowd of Indians—maybe as many as twelve—grabbing at their horses' manes and trying to swing onto their backs. One or two looked like they were cutting the hobbles loose, trying to avoid getting kicked.

The horses had apparently drifted about a hundred yards from the deserted station, and later, the men would guess that the Apaches calculated that was far enough. They were driving the horses across the scrub desert, and to the consternation of Andrews and Wiswall, the horses were making almost as good progress with their hobbles on as if they had been free.

Andrews leveled down with his Sharps and fired. A cloud of dust kicked up beside one of the marauders, but the only other result was that about three of them wheeled toward Andrews and Wiswall, two firing arrows and one aiming what looked like an ancient Enfield rifle.

Andrews and Wiswall hit the dirt as the shafts went over their heads and the shot from the Enfield went wide. Andrews shucked another cartridge into the Sharps as Wiswall, lying prone, opened fire with his Springfield.

The three Indians who had shot at them scattered, and the rest stayed occupied with driving the horses away. By now, a brave straddled each of the three horses, and one of the draft animals was running free, the tattered remains of the leather hobbles flying like a pennant from its off foreleg.

The two rose to chase after the horse thieves but had to immediately dive for cover again as the Indians sent another volley in their direction. Andrews and Wiswall returned fire as best they could, but the cause was lost. Soon the horses and the Apaches were out of range.

Shep had stayed near his masters during the melee, barking up a storm but not giving chase. Keeping a wary eye on the retreating band, the men fell back to the station.

"Well, I'll be damned!" Andrews stared at the barely visible figures hurrying to the south, all that was left to be seen of either animals or Indians by this time. "I should have sidelined those horses! Of all the harebrained ..." He shook his head and spat in disgust.

"Why wouldn't they have just cut the sideline, like they did the hobbles?" Wiswall said. "Once they decided they could get the horses started without our hearing, it was all up, I expect."

"Maybe so," Andrews said in a grudging voice. "At least they didn't get the dog."

"Wonder he wasn't shot," Wiswall said, looking at Shep. "Standing right out there in the open."

They both stared in the direction their horses had gone. "Well … What's our next move, do you think?" Wiswall said.

"I was just trying to decide," Andrews said. "What are we … about a hundred miles from El Paso?"

Wiswall nodded. "And at least seventy-five from Pope's Crossing on the Pecos, if our maps are any good."

"And on foot."

"I don't think we can ride Shep, no."

For the rest of the afternoon, they took turns, one standing watch and the other going through the supplies, trying to decide what might be carried and what had to be left behind. Reasoning that their shortest distance to help lay to the east, they decided to leave the Crow Spring station under cover of darkness and get as far as possible across the broad, flat plain before daylight found them.

They rigged a couple of dummies using their spare clothes and stationed them visibly, arming them with boards that might pass as weapons if seen from sufficient distance. "That ought to slow them down for a while, at least, until they realize that the guards haven't moved in a day or two," Wiswall said, admiring their handiwork.

"I don't expect they'll come back tonight," Andrews said, standing with his hands on his hips as he gazed at the surrounding, barren landscape. "They know the dog will give the alarm if they come near, and they know we're armed. And by morning we'll be as far from here as we can get."

"What about Shep?"

Andrews looked at the dog, at Wiswall, and away, across toward the Guadalupes. "I've got a thought on that," he said, finally. "But none of us is going to like it."

CHAPTER TEN

-

As twilight deepened, Andrews and Wiswall gathered up such wood as could be found around the old enclosure. A couple of watch fires would make the place look more occupied and would aid their deception. They lit the tinder beneath the two miniature pyres and watched as the flames began to lick upward.

With a heavy heart, Andrews called Shep to his side, standing beside the ambulance. When the dog came, he kneeled down and pointed to the bag of corn and the slab of bacon lying on the ground underneath the little wagon.

"Shep, you have to stay here." He patted the ground under the wagon. "You have to stay here until we get back."

The dog nosed the bag of corn and sniffed the bacon, then looked back at Andrews.

"You've got to stay with the stuff. We'll come back for you—with help."

Wiswall looked at the scene for another few seconds, then turned away, swallowing repeatedly.

Shep's tongue flicked out as he licked his chops. He raised his head slightly, testing the air. Then he lay down beside the bag of corn. He continued to watch Andrews.

"God damn those Apaches, anyhow," Wiswall muttered, his back still turned.

Andrews angled his face toward his partner. "Now, where is all that kindness and understanding you were preaching, not so long ago?"

"That was theoretical. This is personal."

Andrews gave a sad smile and turned back toward Shep. "You'll stay, won't you, old friend? Stay here with our stuff until we come back for you. All right?" He scratched the dog under his chin. Shep licked Andrews's hand and lay his head upon his paws.

Andrews dipped a bucketful of water from one of the casks lashed to the side of the Coolidge and set it on the ground beside Shep. "I guess he can get to the corral tank, when this runs out," he said.

It seemed to take forever for full dark to come. The two men loaded themselves up with all the ammunition and weapons they could carry, along with a blanket and a canteen apiece. They each spent a few moments talking in low voices to Shep, who watched their faces but never made a move to get up. The dog's ready acceptance of his lonely and dangerous duty was heartbreaking. Neither of the men thought the other noticed the emotion displayed as they turned from the dog and walked out of the abandoned stage station.

Each thought he was the only one who looked back as they went.

The map indicated a ranch of some sort about fifty miles east, around the south end of the Guadalupe range and across the mesa. The stage road would take them past Pinery Station by morning, and there they would likely find water. They set out, moving along the stage road in the darkness.

The stage road soon became deep with loose sand. It was awful to walk in, and before long, the men were laboring and panting beneath their packloads. By the time they reached the broken ridges fronting the Guadalupe slopes, they were drenched in sweat beneath their coats, despite the steady and cold wind quartering into their faces.

"At least we'll be in among the broken country by sunup," Wiswall panted. "There'll be cover."

The road took them to the right, circumventing the mountains and angling them past El Capitan, the lonely sentinel at the southernmost end of the Guadalupes. The stark, abrupt peak rose in front of them, a darker hulk against the spangled night sky. Rounding El Capitan and keeping to the road, they would come to the ruins of Pinery Station—if they didn't collapse along the way.

As the gray of dawn was coming on, they arrived at a foot trail that angled to the left, disappearing into the rocky saddle that separated El Capitan from Guadalupe Peak. "That looks like going the way we want to go," Andrews said as Wiswall leaned over, hands on his knees, catching his breath.

Wiswall peered up the path as far as he could see in the near-dark. "And it's not out in the open. I'll follow your lead, though I'm not fond of the thought of climbing, right at the moment."

"We'll rest a few minutes and drink a little water, then we'll go," Andrews said.

A ground-hugging, morning fog rolled slowly toward them as the eastern sky began to pink behind the mountains. "It's coming up pretty fast," said Wiswall. "If it reaches us, we'll not be able to see twenty feet in front or behind. It'll either hide us from the Mescaleros, or they'll use it to jump us."

"Well, we'd better get moving, in any case. Or else die standing still."

They straightened themselves, spent a minute or two helping each other adjust their packs and the straps on their rifles, and then began the trudge up the winding, narrow trail that led up into the saddle.

"If we're lucky, this will let us cut the corner off the mountains and come that much sooner to the Pinery station," Andrews said as they picked their way along. "That puts us some twenty miles from that ranch we saw on the map, I'd judge."

"I hope you're right. But I have an uneasy feeling that you and I aren't the first to walk this path."

Andrews said nothing to this, but Wiswall saw his hand stray down to the Colt revolver holstered at his belt. Wiswall checked his sidearm, also.

Since leaving Shep at the Crow Springs station, Andrews and Wiswall had walked some thirty miles. They hadn't paused to eat; unease had curbed their appetites. They huddled into their coats as the winter wind, channeled by the narrow defile through which they passed, bore down on them with what they considered an unnaturally strong interest.

Reaching an opening in the trail, they paused to take in a sweeping panorama of the desert floor that lay on the other side of the saddle they were traversing.

"That's where we're heading" Andrews said, pointing. "I believe this path leads right down to Pine Springs and the Pinery, a mile on. All we have to do now is descend, and get back onto the Butterfield. I calculate we'll soon be more than halfway to the ranch."

"Lord a'mighty, I hope we can get some help there," Wiswall said, wiping his face. "Even one other man who is a fair shot, and three fresh horses. We could have Shep safe in no time."

"One thing at a time," Andrews said. "Let's get to Pinery, rest up under some cover, and refill our canteens. Then we'll see about the rest of it."

They started down the slope that led to the place where, they hoped, the path opened on the plain to the east of the

Guadalupes. Near there they would find what was left of the Pinery station, with water at nearby Pine Spring.

The path wandered back and forth in the manner of any trail that is first made by people on foot, avoiding large boulders and skirting steep slopes as they seek the easiest way. The only sound was that of their boots, striking the rough trail and scuffing along the rocks as they braced themselves backwards for the descent toward the flatlands. Neither of them wanted to think too much about crossing that broad expanse on foot under the glaring light of day, but it was the only way, and they knew it.

The footpath made an abrupt turn that led down into a small draw. Reaching the upslope opening of the draw, the two partners froze, staring dead ahead.

Staring back at them from the opposite end of the draw were what looked like a whole village's-worth of Mescaleros. Three or four of the men were mounted. All were armed.

For an instant, no one moved. And then, Andrews and Wiswall wheeled and ran for all they were worth, back up the trail the way they had come. As they ducked out of the draw back into the defile, they heard arrows clicking against the rocks, near where their heads had been an instant before.

"Is this wide enough for horses?" panted Andrews. "If it is, we can't outrun them."

"There's a sugar loaf butte up to the left!" Wiswall shouted. "If we can get up there we can hold them off, maybe."

Andrews and Wiswall scrambled up the cone-shaped formation, their breath burning in and out of their chests. As they climbed, they could hear the yells and calls of the Apaches, rushing up the trail toward them.

They reached the peak and flung down their packs. "Pull some of these rocks up close," Andrews said. "They'll do for breastworks. You take that side, and I'll cover this one."

The partners crouched behind their impromptu bunkers, readying their rifles. They steadied their breathing and sighted down their barrels, waiting for the first target that might present himself below them. As soon as the leaders came into view, they opened fire.

The Indians quickly scattered off the trail and behind the surrounding boulders. They sent a small swarm of arrows at the two defenders, all of which ricocheted harmlessly off the rocks around them. There was a scattering of gunfire from below that kicked up dust and rock chips near Andrews and Wiswall but otherwise did no damage. Everything grew still—nothing moved.

"Keep a sharp lookout," Wiswall said in a low voice. "They'll be up to something, for sure."

"I think most of them are on your side," Andrews said.

The day was still cool, but perched on the top of the butte, they felt perspiration trickling down their necks and backs. Their eyes relentlessly scoured the slopes below, watching for any sign of their attackers.

A stone's throw down the slope from Andrews, a keg-sized rock scooted upward, grinding against the loose shingle on the hillside. He saw a flicker of movement behind it. "They're pushing rocks up toward us, taking cover behind them," he said quietly. "Trying to slip up on us?"

Wiswall nodded. "I see them over here, too. Four or five of them, in a rough semicircle, working their way upslope. Reckon I ought to try and pick them off?"

"No … wait. Let's let them get closer. Let them think we don't know where they are. And keep looking for anything else they might try."

For a long time, the only sound was the wind, sighing past the rocks. Now and then, one of the partners would see a stone scoot a little bit, then a little bit more. The day crawled slowly past as the duo bided their time, the Apaches trying to tighten the noose around their necks.

As the afternoon light started to bend toward evening, Andrews said, "Get ready. We may have a break over on this side in a minute."

Without taking his eyes from his surveillance, Wiswall slid an arm through one of the straps of his pack. He said, "Just say the word."

As Andrews peered through his gun sight, a dark shape rose ever so slowly over the edge of the rock Andrews had been watching. He exhaled slowly and squeezed the trigger. The Sharps spoke and the head disappeared.

"Now!" Andrews said in a low, urgent voice. "Down this side. I've knocked over one of them."

Crouching low and clutching their rifles, they scrambled and half-fell down the rocky slope. In twenty strides, they passed an Indian, sprawled on his back in a pool of blood and staring sightlessly at the sky, a clean hole in his forehead. They didn't stop running until they were almost to the plain, where they found a hidden crevice that would admit them both. With solid rock at their backs, they crouched in the crevice, pistols cocked, to wait for full dark.

"I guess they thought we would try to get away back down the trail," Wiswall half-whispered as they made ready for the long walk back to Crow Springs. "Only the one you shot was to the west; everybody else was on the other side."

Andrews's face was grim. "We'll recuperate with Shep. Right now, I feel like hiking all night. Leaving him in the first place was the worst feeling I ever knew."

"How many do you think we killed?"

"Probably just the one."

"Well, the rest of them will have their blood up, for sure."

"No help for it, though. Was him or us."

"That's certain."

Night fell. Andrews and Wiswall eased out of their hiding place and began the long walk, back down the Butterfield Trail toward Crow Spring where, they prayed, Shep was still waiting for them.

CHAPTER ELEVEN

Andrews and Wiswall jogged, walked, and stumbled in the dark through the low hills of the western Guadalupe Pass, paralleling the old Butterfield route. They wanted to delay until the last possible moment walking out onto the salt flats. Even in full dark, they felt as if eyes peered out at them from behind every boulder. Once they were out on that plain, with little taller than a man's waist growing on it, they would be completely exposed.

Soon there was nothing else for it; they struck west into the flat. It was overcast, and any other time they would have cursed the lack of a moon. But now, they preferred the concealment, even though it made the going more complicated.

They proceeded almost like blind men, hoping that the bearings they had taken during the fading daylight would carry them across to the abandoned station, or near enough. They took frequent sightings of clumps of bushes or other such landmarks as they could discern in the dark, doing their dead-level best to hew a straight line across to their destination.

They spoke not a word; the only sound of their passing was the scraping of shoe leather and labored breathing. Every so often, by silent agreement, they halted, standing still in the darkness to listen and stretch their eyes vainly into the night for any evidence of pursuit.

They needed to be under cover by daylight. Without question, the Mescaleros could easily track them across the plain. The partners hoped that the Apaches' respect for their superior weaponry would make them pause before attempting the head-on assault of a fortified place—if they could get there.

Andrews and Wiswall were weary beyond weariness as the sky began to turn from black to gray behind them. The only good thing about the rising light was that it revealed the tumbled hulk of the Crow Spring station, huddled in their direction of travel at the utmost limit of their reduced vision. At least they hadn't strayed too far from the route during their trek through the darkness.

"Buck up, partner; we're almost home," Andrews said, shifting his pack and striding forward with what was left of his determination. Wiswall said nothing but followed doggedly.

Suddenly, in the silence and solitude of the desert, they heard the faint but unmistakable sound of a barking dog.

Stopping in his tracks to better listen and hear, Wiswall said, "Do you suppose?"

"Yes, without a doubt!"

They quickened their pace, fatigue forgotten for the moment. As they came nearer to the station, they thought they could discern a small, black shape atop one of the broken walls. It was Shep! He was alive!

By the time they were within a stone's throw of the station, the dog was racing toward them. He met the two weary travelers with tail a-wag, bounding and leaping about them and licking their hands and faces.

"Good to see you too, old friend," Andrews said. Despite the dull aches clenching every square inch of his frame, he couldn't keep the grin off his face. Wiswall, too, was rubbing and petting Shep, chuckling quietly.

As they entered the yard of the station, they saw that the two dummy sentinels remained at their posts. The side of bacon beneath the ambulance was gnawed down to less than half the size it had been when they left, but the bag of corn was mostly untouched. As the light broadened, the partners could discover no evidence that any human foot had trod inside the dilapidated adobe walls since their departure, the night before.

Andrews and Wiswall eased their packs onto the ground and lay their rifles in the bed of the ambulance. Andrews sat heavily on the tongue of the wagon, leaning on his elbows and staring at the ground. All at once, exhaustion dropped onto him like a lead-weighted blanket.

"Why don't you crawl inside the wagon and get a little shut-eye?" Wiswall said. "Shep and I will keep watch. Then you can take over for me."

"Partner, I will not dissuade you. Right this minute, I'd pick sleep over a fresh-grilled steak."

Andrews pulled himself to his feet and clambered in beneath the canvas cover of the Coolidge. Within minutes, he was sawing logs.

By noon, Andrews stirred awake to the smell of freshly brewed coffee. He roused himself and scooted outside to find Wiswall sipping gingerly from a tin cup and eating one of the cold biscuits he had stowed in his pack before they left on their ill-fated expedition to the Pinery station.

Andrews poured coffee into the waiting, empty cup and took a careful sip. "I guess a little fire won't hurt anything," he said.

"Not exactly like our presence is a secret, any more," Wiswall said. "I didn't want to bother you with the stove."

"Much appreciated." He fished through his pack and found his own biscuit. "Any sign?"

"Nothing but a buzzard or two. I hope they don't know something we don't."

Andrews gave a low chuckle. He looked down at the toe of his boot, now separated from the badly worn sole along a two-inch gap. "That little hike was bad for our footwear."

Wiswall took another swallow of coffee and tossed the rest on the ground. "Yep. I've got a heel that's about to come off, and I can feel the pebbles on the ground every time I take a step."

"I don't like to think about peeling my boots off, for fear of seeing what my feet look like," Andrews said. "I also don't like to think about walking back to Ysleta."

Wiswall climbed up onto the wagon and crawled onto one of the cots. "Well, I guess we could ask Victorio's bunch to loan us a couple of ponies."

"I'll wake you when it starts to get dark," Andrews said.

"Or if Victorio happens by."

"That, too."

That evening, with Shep curled on the ground between them and giving every evidence of contentment, the two men talked, low-voiced in the dark. They recapitulated everything that had happened to them from the theft of their horses to their narrow escape from the Mescalero band.

Now that they had gotten away from the immediate danger and recovered from the worst of their fatigue, they had the luxury of considering their situation and their options. It was not an encouraging inventory.

"Why do you reckon they didn't come back here?" Wiswall said.

Andrews shook his head. "Maybe the horses were mainly what they were after, and they didn't calculate the rest was worth the risk. Or maybe they just had other fish to fry. I don't hold myself as much of an expert on how Apaches think."

"Do you really think we ought to head for Ysleta?"

"It's either that or wait here for a patrol to come along," Andrews said. "And you heard from both the army and the Rangers about how likely that is."

After a long silence, Wiswall said, "Do you reckon we could wait one more day to start out?"

Andrews stared into the dark. "Yes. Let's rest up tonight and tomorrow, as best we can. Then at dark tomorrow, we'll strike out. If we can make it as far as the Cornudas, we can lay up during the day."

They both looked down at Shep. After another long silence, Wiswall said, "I'll take the first watch with Shep. Go ahead and lie down."

The next morning, they scrounged among the supplies in their wagon and found some gunny sacks they could use to bind up their dilapidated boots. With a little luck, this might carry them to Ysleta.

"Of course, if the Apaches get to us, we won't need boots anymore," Andrews commented grimly.

"Make me a promise, partner," Wiswall said. "If it becomes truly hopeless, put a bullet between my eyes before you do the same for yourself. That seems preferable to me to enduring the tortures we've been told they inflict on their captives."

"I've had the same thought. You can depend on me for that last mercy."

"And you, me."

Several feet away, Shep's head snapped to alertness. The men grabbed their rifles.

They saw a blurred line of motion in the far, gray distance, back toward the Guadalupe Mountains. "Herd of pronghorns on the move," Andrews said, after several seconds of quiet study.

They eased the firearms back down to the ground beside the place where they sat and resumed fashioning their makeshift footwear: wrapping the gunny sacks around their boots and binding them in place with cord.

"I allow these fancy stockings will make us harder to track, at least," Wiswall offered. "I don't imagine our trail will much resemble that of a walking man."

"I don't imagine our feet will much resemble such, either, by the time we come to Ysleta."

For the rest of the day, they ate such of their supplies as they could make ready with no fire and packed what they could into their traveling bags. As the dull gray sky began to dim, they sat on their packs, contemplating what lay before them.

"I suppose it would be too much to ask for the rain to hold off until we make it back." Wiswall said.

"I'd rather walk in the rain if it keeps the Mescaleros in their wikiups and our scalps on our heads."

"Fair enough." After a long silence, Wiswall said, "I guess we'll leave him here again?"

"I don't see any other way, do you? If he barks, he'll give us away. The same if he runs out in front of us; why else would a dog be out in the middle of this country?"

"I reckon it's so. But I hate it, all the same."

"You and me both."

Dark came, and once again, the men gave their dog his orders. They each spent some minutes with him, talking in low tones as they scratched him behind the ears and patted along his back. And when they turned to walk away into the night, down the old stage trail, Shep, as he had done before, stood watching them go, but made no offer to follow.

"It sticks hard in my throat, leaving him," Wiswall said as they shuffled away from the Crow Spring station. "Even if this works the way we plan, we'll be gone for several days before we can get back here."

Andrews said nothing.

CHAPTER TWELVE

They trudged along the trail, ascending toward the low, barren hills of the Cornudas range, less than thirty miles away. They saw no reason not to follow the old stage trail; it was the surest way to avoid getting lost and, by walking at night when Victorio's people were presumably denned up, they thought they might actually make the best time possible.

Arriving at the Cornudas before dawn, they considered making camp in the deserted stage station, but reasoned that if the Mescaleros were hunting them, it would be the first place they would look. So, instead, the partners scrambled up into the rough granite formations of the hills and found themselves a shelter amid the rocks that would hide them from any prying eyes. As at the Huecos, they found plenty of cached rainwater in the natural cups and basins of the rocks, and they drank as much as they could hold before filling their canteens.

The beds in their hiding place were hard and rocky, but the men were so desperately weary that whoever wasn't on watch slept like the dead. They passed the day alternating between watching and sleeping, and as night came on they readied themselves for the tramp across to the Huecos, some twenty miles across the Diablo Plateau.

A light rain fell on them, off and on, until about midnight. Even when the rain stopped, a cold north wind drove the clouds across the moon. They huddled as deep in their coats and slickers as they could, but the wind found its way in, chilling them to the bone as they made their way along on sore, bleeding feet.

An hour or so before dawn on the second night back toward Ysleta, they spotted a small ledge off a rocky crest among large boulders overlooking the Hueco Bolson, west of the tanks. With difficulty, they climbed up to the ledge and scooted back in under it as far as they could go. They passed another night like the one they had just had, except that they both admitted it was much harder to keep watch, as exhaustion pressed their eyelids closed with a force that was no less irresistible for its subtlety.

The brief nap the two eagerly sought turned into a full, sound, long overdue night's sleep. They hadn't planned to oversleep but now didn't regret it. From their slight rocky perch in the first light of sunrise, the two observed the desert below them, all shimmering in whites and silvers in a light fog, as far as their eyes could see.

Nearing the end of the next night's dreary tramp across Hueco Bolson, Andrews said, "How do you figure? Are we far enough west that we might risk traveling in daylight? If we did, we could reach Fort Bliss before nightfall tomorrow, I calculate."

Chewing on a mouthful of dried beef, Wiswall said, "I'm so tuckered out that if Victorio showed up right now, I don't think I could even muster the strength to trot in the other direction. If you're willing to try it, I am, too."

"That's settled, then. We'll rest up for a little while when daylight comes, and then we'll keep moving. The more ground we can cover, the sooner we'll get back to Ysleta."

"Hot coffee, hot food, warm beds, and maybe a few hours of sleep. Then, we go back and get our dog. That's all I want."

By dawn, the temperature had dropped below freezing. Andrews and Wiswall huddled out of the wind in a mesquite-bordered ravine and tried to rest. Soon, though, they had to admit that they were too cold.

"I expect we'll do better if we keep moving," Andrews said. "If we did manage to go to sleep in this cold, we might not wake up."

"Lead on; I'll go as far as these battered feet will carry me. The sooner we get where we're going, the better I'll like it."

By mid-afternoon, and in relatively clear—though still cold—weather, Andrews and Wiswall were ambling past the outlying haciendas to the east of El Paso del Norte. Here and there, sheep scattered across the landscape, seemingly impervious to the cold wind that tormented the weary hikers.

Flat-roofed, sandstone dwellings began to dot the countryside, each with its beehive-shaped, adobe horno behind, giving out thin wisps of smoke. Acequia-bordered fields, brown and fallow for the winter, came into view.

By late afternoon they came to Fort Bliss, on the northeast side of the city. They hailed the first sentry they saw and begged for aid. The soldier took one look at the weary, battered travelers and immediately beckoned to one of his fellows. "I can't leave my station, but you'd better get these men in out of the cold. They look like they're fixing to fall over any minute now."

They were taken to the enlisted men's barracks, though they protested every step of the way that they needed to see Major Osbourne. Within half an hour, they were both lying in tubs of heated water, and twenty minutes after that, they lay on cots under thick, woolen blankets, dead to the world.

They woke the next morning to find clean clothes lying beside their cots. These consisted of rather worn and dated uniforms with all the insignia removed, but they were warm, and Andrews and Wiswall donned them gladly. They bandaged their feet as best they could and slid them, with many a grimace, into the Army brogans they found waiting for them, along with the clothes.

The victuals with which they broke their fast might have been considered bland in other circumstances, but the starved travelers wolfed down the eggs, bacon, and toasted bread as if they hadn't seen food in a month.

"Major Osborne is waiting for you in his office," an orderly told them as Andrews and Wiswall returned their empty plates and utensils for washing by the enlisted men's kitchen detail.

They found the major in the same place they had met with him before, when he had agreed to sell them the Coolidge. "Gentlemen, it seems that you have had a rough go of it," he said as soon as they had all shaken hands and sat down. "I regret to remind you that I indicated such might be the case if you went east on the old stage road."

"Yes, and your prophecy came true in almost every detail," Andrews said with a sad smile. "Victorio's people are the richer for it by three horses, and we are the poorer by most of our supplies and our dog."

"I'm not happy to hear it," Osbourne said. He then urged them to give him the most complete narrative possible of all that had transpired since they had left Ysleta, all those days before.

When they were finished, Osbourne made a number of pointed inquiries about their encounters with the Mescaleros: asking them to repeat where they had first made contact, how many were in the band they encountered in the Guadalupe mountains, what sort of weaponry they observed among the Indians, and other queries on tactical matters.

When they had answered all the major's questions, he sank into thought for several seconds. He looked up at them then, and said, "What are your plans now?"

"As soon as we can, we mean to go back and get our dog," Andrews said. "We were hoping for some aid from the army."

Osbourne looked at them and shook his head slowly. "Mr. Andrews and Mr. Wiswall, with all due respect, we have already plowed this ground, once before. This is an infantry command; we have no cavalry here."

"Indeed," Andrews said, "and yet, we find it prudent to make the request, at least."

"Noted. And my answer remains the same; I will not risk the lives of my men for no other reason than to retrieve a dog—one that ought not to be where he is in the first place, if you take my meaning."

"I understand you, Major," Andrews said. "And if you will inform us what we owe the government for our room and board, we will settle our accounts and inquire elsewhere."

The major's face softened a trifle. "There will be no charge for the small comforts we have provided you." He drummed his fingers on the desk for a second or two. "I don't suppose I can persuade you against what you mean to do?"

"I'm afraid not, Major."

Osbourne sighed and shook his head. "Very well, then. As before, I suppose you may as well inquire of Baylor and his Rangers, over at Ysleta."

"I believe we will do just that. Might we borrow the use of a couple of horses? We have had about all the walking our health will stand, these last few days."

"Never mind that. I'll have my sergeant major drive you over there as soon as you are ready to go."

CHAPTER THIRTEEN

-

As the master sergeant drove Andrews and Wiswall through the central streets of El Paso, the sky began to clabber. By the time they reached the gates in Ysleta, they were slumped beneath their slickers as a cold rain arrowed in from the northwest. The partners bailed out of the buckboard in the downpour and splashed up the steps onto the porch of Baylor's dwelling and headquarters.

Straightaway, a man standing on the porch said to them, "Weren't you fellows here a few days ago? Where's that big, fine shepherd dog you had with you?"

"That's why we need to speak to Lieutenant Baylor. Is he in the vicinity?"

"He went over to the livery on some business, but I expect him back any time," the Ranger said. "That's why I'm waiting for him here."

Another Ranger strolled over. "You're the fellows that set out on the old Butterfield road, aren't you? How far did you get? Is the dog all right?"

By the time the company's commander arrived, just a few minutes later, a crowd of Rangers had gathered around Andrews and Wiswall to listen to the story of their experiences of the last few days. Baylor stood at the edge of the group for a minute or two, then waded through, coming up the steps to where the partners stood.

"Come on inside, gentlemen. Let's have the whole story, from start to finish. And I'll especially want to know why Shep isn't by your side …"

Once inside his office with Andrews and Wiswall, Baylor grabbed the chair from behind his desk and motioned Andrews and Wiswall to a leather couch along the wall.

"I'm relieved you two are safe. I gather you had a run-in with some of Victorio's people. How far did you get? All of us figured you were already pale in death by now. So, tell me!"

Andrews narrated their recent history in as much detail as he could summon, beginning with their departure and ending with their exhausting walk back from Crow Spring. Baylor's eyes bored into both of them as Andrews spoke.

When Andrews finished, the lieutenant sat quiet for several seconds. "Well, that's some story. But thank God, you're safe now." Baylor got up and walked to his office door, motioning for his guests to keep their seats. They heard him give an indistinct order to someone outside, whereupon he came back in.

"So you left Shep in command of the station, did you? And like a good and faithful soldier, he stayed at his post." Baylor shook his head slowly, a look of deep admiration on his face. "Gentlemen, that dog is one in a million."

"You cannot possibly imagine how it tore us to leave him," Andrews said. "And yet, what else could we do? If he came with us, he was almost certain to betray our presence to watching eyes or listening ears."

"Just so," Baylor said, nodding. "I would likely have done much the same, if our positions had been exchanged."

The door opened, and Sergeant Gillett came in. "Thank you for coming, sergeant," Baylor said. "I trust you remember Mr. Andrews and Mr. Wiswall?"

Gillett nodded at the men. "I hear you've had quite a time of it, here of late."

"True enough," Andrews said.

"We were just talking about that fine shepherd dog of theirs," Baylor said.

"Yes, Shep. I wondered where he was," Gillett said.

"Well, that's why we've come to see you, Lieutenant. We intend to go back and get him, one way or another. We applied to Major Osbourne, out at Fort Bliss, but it was a waste of time. He won't help us, he says, because he has only infantry, not cavalry. I gave the dog my word, and the word of Wiswall here, that we would go back and get him, and that means as much to me as if I had said it to a man. If you don't go with us, we aim to go alone, just as soon as we can buy or borrow some horses." Andrews looked at Wiswall, then back at Baylor and Gillett. "We're going within the hour, sir, one way or another. We'll go alone, but we'd surely like to have some help."

Baylor stared hard at Andrews.

"We left him a slab of bacon and half a sack of corn, five days ago. When we last saw him two days ago, everything was half eaten. If the coyotes, the rain and cold, or the Apaches don't get him, he's going to starve to death, because he won't leave the wagon after I asked him to stay. Mr. Andrews, Mr. Wiswall, surely you remember me telling you how dangerous it was to go to the Pecos along the Butterfield route?"

After a long silence, Andrews said, "Lieutenant, we have some money. If that isn't enough, I'm willing to work off the debt, here in El Paso."

"That goes for me, too," Wiswall said.

Baylor studied them for a moment, then turned to look out the window. The rain pattered against the panes, and all Andrews and Wiswall could think of was their poor dog, probably hunkered beneath the ambulance—if it was still there—staring miserably out at a hostile landscape.

"You are asking us to ride into considerable danger; I assume you appreciate that," Baylor said at last, turning back to look at them. "As you now have learned, Victorio and his braves might be anywhere in the country east of here. Further, your going has alerted them. And you have killed one of his men."

They silently returned Baylor's look. "We are sensible of the situation, yes," Andrews said, finally. "And we will understand completely if you choose to deny our plea."

Baylor nodded slowly. "And yet, you will still go back there."

"We will," Wiswall said immediately. Andrews nodded.

Baylor stared at them a long while. Very slowly, a smile crept across his face. "Well, gentlemen, I can't fault your grit, at least. I believe I'm going with you." He turned toward his sergeant. "Assemble all the men in the outer office, now." Gillett went out.

"We'll soon find out if any of the other men here will accompany us. We'll leave as soon as we're outfitted for the journey."

Within a minute or two, they heard the sound of boots scuffing across the floor in the outer office. "Shall we go and present our case?" Baylor said. He stepped to the door and opened it, motioning Andrews and Wiswall through.

As the men gathered, several sidled over to Andrews and Wiswall and asked, in half-whispers, about Shep's whereabouts. They answered as briefly as they could, until they were interrupted by Baylor's voice, from the front of the room.

"Our friends here had trouble with the Apaches. Their horses were stolen at the old Crow Spring station at the foot of the Guadalupes, halfway to the Pecos. They walked back here with gunny sacks over their shoes.”

There was a low murmur. A few of the Rangers glanced at Andrews and Wiswall with something like respect in their eyes.

“They had to leave Shep behind because he might innocently have given them away. And we all know what happens to people who get caught by Victorio.

“They’ve already been to the fort and were denied help because all Bliss has over there is foot soldiers. Now, they are standing here, asking if anyone will go back with them into an Apache-infested area to retrieve the ambulance and fetch Shep, if he’s still alive.”

If the room was quiet before, it was now as silent as a tomb.

“Now, I realize that not one of you has been in the service for more than three months. Miller, you joined us four days ago. Seaburn, you enrolled and took your oath eleven days back. The rest of you have been with me since December first, just past. None of us draw enough pay to justify riding into country where you may well meet with several hundred renegade Apaches.

“Be that as it may, I’m going with these men to retrieve that ambulance and their Shep. I will not ask any of you to join us. I love life as much as the next man, and will not give it up easily. But for that particular dog, I am willing to risk it, as I would for any good friend who is hurting. We’re leaving in one hour, after we pack up. We should make the Tanks by tonight, Crow Spring the next day, if we ride at a trot. My hope is that the weather and the Apaches behave. If any of you choose to join us—"

"With all due respect, Lieutenant, we're wasting time," one of the men said. He looked around at the others for a moment. "Let's go, boys." He walked out the door.

Another man started for the door . "I'll get the horses saddled and start sacking up the feed."

Then another Ranger said, "We'll likely need the mules and the packsaddles." He followed the other two outside.

Another Ranger turned toward Andrews and Wiswall with a broad grin. "You two fellows have walked a hundred miles in this weather with shoe leather worn down to sandpaper. I reckon I can ride with you at least as far as Crow Spring."

"Well, I'll not let it be said that I let a good dog freeze to death if I could help it," another one said as he started for the door.

Andrews and Wiswall stared about them with jaws hanging slack.

Baylor grinned at Gillett. "Well, Sergeant, looks like you're the one to stay behind and watch over the place."

"Begging your pardon, sir, but like hell I will!"

Baylor laughed. "Well, we need to leave somebody here to watch the place."

"How about the two married ones? Burnes and Thomas?"

"Yes, that'll do. The other nine of us will go, and we need to bring scouts. Sergeant, can you go and summon Simon?"

"Yes, sir." Gillett left. Andrews and Wiswall remained alone in the room with Baylor.

"Lieutenant, what, precisely, just happened here? Do I correctly understand that every one of your men has volunteered to go with us to retrieve our dog?"

"I believe that is correct," Baylor said, a little smile playing about his lips.

"And they understand the danger?" Wiswall said.

"They have learned well that Victorio is not to be trifled with, yes."

Andrews and Wiswall both stood dumbstruck. "We came here to make just such a request," Andrews said finally, "yet hardly dared to hope that even one or two Rangers would return with us. I think I can speak for my partner, here, as well as myself … and yet I cannot find the words to adequately say what we are feeling."

"Well, that's all right," Baylor said. "Leave the words for later. Right now, we had best prepare for action."

CHAPTER FOURTEEN

-

Andrews and Wiswall trailed Baylor to the barracks, carrying their rifles and ammunition. The Ranger commander asked for two horses to be brought around for them, and another man who was serving as quartermaster for the expedition pointed them toward a couple of worn, but sturdy-looking saddles.

The main door to the barracks swung open, and five figures dimmed the entrance as they stepped across the threshold. The Tiguas came in, wrapped in furs and cradling Winchesters in the crooks of their arms. Broad-brimmed, brown felt hats, each decorated with a feather or two, were jammed low on their heads.

Baylor greeted them gravely. "Sergeant Olguin, thank you for coming on such quick notice. But Simon, you did not need to bring your brothers. This will not be an easy ride, or a safe one."

"That is why they come," the Tigua leader said. "I tell them what the sergeant has said. They say if I go, they go."

Baylor turned to the partners and beckoned them forward. "Mr. Andrews, Mr. Wiswall, please meet Simon Olguin, our chief scout. You heard me call him 'sergeant,' and he has earned that rank many times over."

Andrews was uncertain as to the custom for greeting an Indian, especially one who carried such a palpable air of authority as Simon Olguin. His dark eyes swept over Andrews's face, then did the same for Wiswall's standing at his partner's shoulder. He inclined his head perhaps two inches; Andrews and Wiswall did the same.

"These are his brothers," Baylor continued, "Bernardo, Ponciano, and Francisco. And this is Domingo, son of Bernardo. There are no finer scouts, trackers, or fighters between San Antonio and Arizona."

"Mr. Olguin, we are very grateful for your help," Andrews said. "You are putting yourself into a good deal of trouble on our account."

"The lieutenant calls. We come," Olguin said.

The Tiguas wore homespun woolen trousers with buckskin leggings laced up to the knee. They stood in heelless moccasins with calico kerchiefs wrapped around their heads, just visible beneath their hats. Each had a single-edged Bowie knife slung at his waist, and long cartridge belts crisscrossed their chests.

"Simon, here, and his older brother, Bernardo, the tall one next to him, are the backbones, the sturdiest members of the Pueblo Tigua tribe in the Ysleta locality," Baylor said. "These men have kept all of us out of some mighty tough scrapes, I can tell you."

Someone called that the horses were ready, and Andrews and Wiswall, along with the Rangers, hoisted their tack and went outside. Gillett fell in beside them.

"Simon is the Tiguas' tribal war captain, and, in my opinion, the smartest of them all," the sergeant said. "He speaks for all of them, brothers included. He told me that he is going all the way with us, but the three brothers and the young one are only going to accompany us up to the Tanks."

Andrews and Wiswall slung their saddles and blankets across the backs of two ponies Gillett pointed out to them. They cinched and buckled, then fitted the bridles on their mounts after easing the bits between their jaws. Someone handed Wiswall a saddle holster for his Springfield. Andrews motioned away the one held toward him. "The Sharps is too long for that holster. I'll manage without it."

Someone led out two mules, and others began lashing on the supplies they would carry for the convoy: extra ammunition, sacks of grain for the animals, tents, kettles, a couple of fowling pieces, spare tack, sacks of dried beef, coffee, and other needful articles.

"Simon and his brothers will ride ahead, behind, and on our flanks all the way to the Tanks," Baylor announced, lifting his voice above the din. "Simon believes the most likely place for trouble is at sunup tomorrow, when we'll be at Hueco."

"Why would that be?" Wiswall said.

"Sometimes, they'll creep and crawl along the high shelves and into the rocky defiles around a camp," Gillett explained. "They'll hide until first light, then swarm over you all at once. But Simon and his people will scout every inch of the canyons for any hint of moccasin or horse tracks."

"I reckon they have a pretty good idea of how the Mescaleros think," Andrews said.

Gillett nodded. "That's why Lieutenant Baylor was glad to see him."

"Why aren't they all going to Crow Spring?" asked Andrews.

"That is Simon Olguin's wish. They would go, but Simon is worried about this patrol, even if he won't say so. If all 300 of Victorio's Apaches take the field against us, how long can we hold out? Those four are the next leaders of the Tiguas; Simon won't let them go all the way on this patrol."

By the time Gillett had finished his explanation, Andrews and Wiswall wore the most somber faces they had owned since losing their horses to the raiders, days before. They mounted up and watched as Simon Olguin and his kin vaulted onto their blanket-clad ponies. The Tigua looked at Baylor.

"All right, men," the lieutenant said. "Let's ride."

CHAPTER FIFTEEN

By the time they were lined out on the road leaving Ysleta, the thick clouds that had threatened rain all through the morning were drifting southwest, pushed by a cold wind that hit the men smack in their faces. They would cut across the desert and pick up the Butterfield trail a mile or two east of Fort Bliss. Glancing back at the low, adobe houses slowly disappearing behind them, Andrews recalled to Wiswall how they had made light of the rude little town and its sparse amenities.

"Well, right this minute, El Paso del Norte looks like home, sweet home," Wiswall said. "Given the choice between staying right here and going where we're going, I could make a snug little life hereabout."

The partners noticed that the men of the Frontier Battalion exercised considerable individuality in their selection of trail and battle equipment; there was very little about their traveling companions that appeared to be standard issue. Many of the Rangers rode with two Winchester rifles holstered by their saddles. Most carried bedrolls lashed at the back of the cantle. Some had a small pannier of hardtack tied on behind. Most had rawhide or hemp lariats looped over the saddle horn. Each Ranger, of course, wore a waist holster with at least one pistol; some carried a brace. All had small leather pouches or wallets in a breast pocket or tied on a rawhide thong that they used to carry salt, tobacco, or additional ammunition. Everything was rigged for maximum portability and efficiency.

"Do you notice their faces?" Andrews said softly. "All so relaxed and natural, as if we're headed for a school meeting and barbecue."

Wiswall nodded, looking around him. "These are damned fine men, every one of them."

Gillett reined up beside them. The mules ambled along just ahead, and Gillett pointed to the packs they carried and explained where the extra pistols, knives, and munitions were located.

"How much road will we cover today, Sergeant?" Andrews asked.

"If we ride double file at an easy trot, we'll be at the Tanks by sundown, depending upon how soft the trail is."

"If this wind holds up, the road ought to dry some," Wiswall said.

"Have you gone often to Hueco Tanks, Sergeant Gillett?" Andrews asked.

"A few times. But I don't especially like it. All those names and pictures, put there by people long gone … I don't know. The place has a poor effect on my imagination, I reckon.

"But it's different for Simon Olguin and his people. The Tiguas consider the hills and rocks there sacred. To Victorio and the Apaches, the Tanks are nothing more than a watering hole, but I've heard it said that the Tiguas gather there to worship."

"Well, if you've got to die, I calculate it's best to die in church," Wiswall said.

"Sergeant, please forgive my friend's gallows humor," Andrews said, shaking his head.

Gillett chuckled. "I've heard worse, Mr. Andrews, I can promise you."

The sergeant gave them a bit of the history of the Tigua people of Ysleta Pueblo. They had come there some two hundred years before, he told them, accompanying Spaniards retreating from a revolt among the Pueblo people up around Santa Fe. "They named their village here Ysleta del Sur—Island of the South—after the place they had come from up in New Mexico, which was also named Isleta."

"They certainly seem stalwart men," Andrews said.

Gillett nodded. "None better."

A few rays of sunlight penetrated the broken clouds as they neared the junction with the Butterfield trail; the men could feel perspiration dampening the collars of their shirts.

Here and there, Rangers began peeling back layers of garments, bundling them and tying them to their saddles as the convoy jogged along at a posting trot.

Coming to the junction, they angled right, heading northeast along the old Butterfield road, riding two abreast. The Tigua scouts peeled away from the rest, taking up positions ahead, behind, and flanking the Rangers. Simon Olguin rode 150 to 200 yards ahead of the party.

By the time they had ridden into the mid-afternoon, the only other humans they had seen were two Mexicans in separate ox carts, both apparently headed for Ysleta, loaded with firewood. Gillett speculated that they had likely come from Sierra Alto, some twenty-four miles from Ysleta. This boded well, he said: If Victorio's warriors had been nearby—say, in the area of the Tanks—these two woodcutters would likely be deceased and their animals butchered.

"Last month," he said, "Victorio's warriors ambushed a small hay encampment not far south of Ysleta. That night, the lieutenant, myself, and nine other Rangers left immediately for the site, stopping at San Elizario to pick up a guide.

"At dawn, we arrived at the spot of the slaughter and picked up the Apaches' trail; it led across the Rio Grande into Mexico. We crossed the river, and twenty-three Mexicans from a little place called Guadalupe joined us in the search. The Sierra Ventana is mighty hard country, and the raiders ambushed us as we were trailing through a canyon.

"Well, we were pretty well pinned down, and after a long fight we decided we had to fall back. We managed to get back to Guadalupe without losing anyone, and the people there welcomed us for the night."

"So Victoria goes back and forth across the Rio Grande pretty much as he wishes?" Andrews said.

Gillett nodded. "We've chased him on both sides, but somehow, he stays a jump ahead of us—and the militias over in Mexico.

"Just last November, two months ago now, none of us knew where Victorio was hiding. He'd been leading both the US and Mexican armies on a merry chase, both north and south of the river. Then he bushwhacked that group of Mexican workers, fifteen or twenty of them. A second party went to the rescue and he killed them, too."

They rode a while without speaking; the only sounds were their mounts' hoofs striking the trail and the squeaking of saddle leather. "Why do you think Victorio does what he does?" Wiswall said, finally.

Gillett stared into the distance for a long time without answering. "I reckon it's in his blood. The Apaches were bred for fighting, and it's what they do best." He turned to Wiswall. "Did you know that they don't call themselves 'Apaches?' They refer to themselves as 'Nideh,' which means 'the people' in their language. 'Apache' is what the neighboring tribes call them. It means, 'people who fight us all the time.'" He gave a low chuckle, shaking his head.

"So, you would say that Victorio's violence is just in his blood? You don't think it has anything to do with what he found on that reservation the government moved him to?" Wiswall said.

Gillett's face hardened. "I don't go in much for politics, Mr. Wiswall. I was hired by the State of Texas to do a job, and I mean to do it."

Wiswall looked like he was about to reply, but Andrews gave him a tight shake of the head. Wiswall looked away, across the arid, gray landscape.

The weather behaved during the remaining hours prior to sunset. In the dimming light of the afternoon, the Ranger convoy arrived at the ramshackle remains of the Hueco Tanks station. Riders began dismounting; two or three men started unloading the mule packs while others gathered kindling and firewood.

"We're here a little earlier than I expected," Lieutenant Baylor said. "Let's make camp and secure the horses around that overhang, right over there." He pointed to a low cut in the cliff, cast in a golden glow by the last rays of the evening sun.

"By the way, I suppose you all have noticed the mounted lookout, on the shoulder of the hill to the northeast?"

The men around Andrews and Wiswall nodded their heads, but both quickly turned and stared in the direction Baylor had indicated. Sure enough, perhaps a quarter-mile distant and well above them, a man sitting a pony was silhouetted against the skyline, apparently staring down at them as they made camp.

From behind Andrews came Simon Olguin's voice. "Not one. Three." The Tigua scout motioned to points in the hills both ahead of and behind them.

"I expect Victorio will know where we are before sunup," Baylor said. "So I don't need to tell you about staying vigilant tonight. Once we're dug in here, he'll lose men in a fight, and he knows it. But we've got eyes on us, and we will have, most likely, until we've finished what we came to do." Baylor glanced up at the watcher visible above them, then back at the men. "We'll be heading out tomorrow morning while it's still dark."

They suppered on boiled, sundried tripe, hardtack, and hot coffee. The Rangers worked out sentry shifts, with some guarding the animals as others warded the perimeter. As he ate dinner, Wiswall leaned over to Andrews. "I don't see Simon Olguin or any of his kinfolk."

Andrews angled his head toward the rocks rising above them. "I expect they're up there … somewhere."

CHAPTER SIXTEEN

Twilight slowly coalesced into the solid black of an overcast winter night. The seven Rangers not on sentry duty cocooned in their bedrolls around the dwindling campfire.

Sergeant Gillett arranged his sleeping place, carefully scooping out a slight depression for his hips before spreading his woolen blankets on the ground. Andrews, still seated on his bedroll, said, "I don't see how you fellows ride for nine hours, sleep on the ground, and then get up in the morning and do it all again the next day—and the day after that."

Gillett smiled and shrugged. "It's the life we signed up for," he said. "Now, mind, I'm not at all opposed to sleeping on a feather mattress. But as often as not, there's something bracing about a night spent in the open, eating food you cooked yourself over a campfire." He peered out into the night for a moment. "Of course, it adds considerably to the enjoyment when you don't have to wonder if 300 or so Mescaleros are about to try to lift your scalp while you sleep."

In the dark, one of the horses gave a low nicker. Andrews could see the dim glow of a pipe ember, coming from a nearby dark bundle that marked the resting place of a Ranger.

"Tell me, gentlemen, if you will," Gillett said as he crawled into his blankets and arranged them about him, "how you came to have Shep. He's a fine dog, but as I watched him when you were with us before, I sensed he had a story to tell."

A soft snore came from the ground beside Andrews; Wiswall had already succumbed to the weariness of the day's trail. "Well, since my partner appears to be asleep," Andrews said softly, "I reckon I can tell you about it."

"How's that? Why does it matter if he's asleep?"

"You'll see." Andrews fished his clay pipe out of one shirt pocket and pinched some tobacco from a pouch in the other. He leaned over to fish a slowly burning twig from the edge of the campfire and blew on it until the end glowed. Touching the red spark to his pipe, he puffed the tobacco into life. He took a long, deep draw as he leaned back on an elbow, facing Gillett.

"As you know, we were coming down from Colorado, aiming to buy burros in Texas and sell them back up in Ouray County, where we come from. We were most of the way through Oklahoma Territory, and we stopped at Fort Sill. You ever been there?"

"Can't say I have," Gillett said.

"Well, I'll tell you, I don't care if I ever see that place again." Andrews took another deep pull on his pipe. "Most of the time—I'd say nearly one hundred percent of the time, actually—the men you run into on the US Army's premises are good enough sorts. About like the general run of the population, mind you, but mostly hardworking, honest men who are trying to do their duty.

"But at Sill … I don't know what it was, sergeant, but I don't think I've ever seen as many shiftless, haphazard cusses in the same place at the same time."

Gillett gave a soft chuckle.

"The one thing that seemed to genuinely interest them was fighting—or watching a fight. And if they couldn't locate a scrape naturally, they'd figure out a way to invent one.

"We could scarcely get out of there quick enough to suit us, Wiswall and I. And on the day we were planning to shake the dust off our feet and ride on to the Red River, we came across the pit."

"The what?"

"Some of the enlisted louts—I hate to call them 'men'— had built a kind of pen, with walls maybe ten, twelve feet high. Big, thick timbers, stood on end, nailed together with planks. Like a small corral, only with solid walls."

"Like something you'd pen a bear in, sounds like," Gillett said.

"You are very close. When we saw the thing, we also saw a crowd of those ne'er-do-wells gathered around, laughing, drinking, and swearing, with money changing hands. We soon surmised that some sort of rowdy wager was afoot.

"We walked closer—should have known better—and in a pitiful shed behind the crowd, six or seven mangy, sorry-looking mutts were tied up. We watched and listened long enough to figure out that these rascals had somehow captured a cougar that they kept penned in their pit; they were throwing stray dogs in there, one at a time, betting on how long it took the cougar to rip the poor beasts apart."

Gillett made a disgusted sound. "I've got no use for wanton cruelty—to man or beast. Surely the officers didn't know what was going on?"

"I doubt it. From what we could tell, the enlisted men had been running their little game for some time, but on the sly, as it were. And, as it occurred during off-duty time, likely the officers didn't make it their business."

Gillett shook his head.

"At any rate, when we got among the crowd, one of them was leading a wretched-looking black shepherd: dirty, feeble, and gaunt from obvious neglect. The poor beast was limping on his off foreleg and whimpering, his tail curled up under him in fear. And yet he went forward willingly; the scoundrel leading him didn't even have to drag him toward his fate.

"As the handler, attended by one or two others with clubs and pistols, opened the gate of the pit, the others clustered around eye-level viewing ports on the sides, eager to see their blood-sport played out. The handler pulled the dog inside, yanked the loop from his neck, and skeedaddled back out as the others slammed the gate closed.

"And that's when Wiswall here sprang into action," Andrews said, glancing down at his slumbering partner. "He yelled out, 'Like hell you will!' and charged for the gate they had just closed. One fellow had the misfortune to be in his path, and he was knocked winding for his trouble. You may not have noticed, Sergeant, but Mr. Wiswall is built approximately like an oak stump."

Gillett chuckled softly in the dark.

"He flung open the gate and dashed inside. By this time, I divined what he was up to and hopped to second him, mostly to guard against mischief from the would-be lion-baiters.

"The dog was cowering just inside the gate, urinating into the dust in terror. The cougar was crouched across the way, bunching up to spring. Wiswall kneeled down beside the dog and, keeping his eyes on the big cat, started talking in low, soothing sounds to the frightened animal."

"Lord a'mighty!" Gillett said softly. "That was mighty cool-headed, I'll allow."

"I'll never forget it," Andrews said. "He stared at that cougar and talked to that dog as if the two of them were in a parlor by the fireplace. And then I heard him say, 'Come on, now fellow. It's time to get you out of this hellhole.' And Wiswall stood up and backed toward the gate—me watching the cougar and the rabble, by turns—and the dog came right along with him, just as if he understood every blessed word Wiswall had said. In fact, I will confess that maybe he did— and still does.

"Well, Sergeant, we walked through that crowd of no-goods, and not a one of the sorry lot laid so much as a finger on the dog or either one of us—especially if they caught a good look at Wiswall's expression. The dog came right along with us, and he has been with us ever since. We've taken care of him, fed him, fussed over him, and talked to him. He has been our constant companion. And I'll say it again; I believe that Shep understood everything Wiswall said to him in that cougar pit, and I believe he understands what we tell him to this day."

Gillett gave a low whistle. "That's a story I'll not soon forget."

"And so you can see two things from this, Sergeant," Andrews said. "First, when we told Shep to stay with our supplies at Crow Spring until we came back for him, he took that as an order, just as surely as you would receive an order from Lieutenant Baylor. It came near to breaking our hearts to leave him, but leave him we did. And that's why we have to go back for him—with or without Major Osbourne's infantry, with or without you and your fellow Rangers, come hell or high water … though I'm mighty glad Lieutenant Baylor agreed to help us out."

There was a long silence. Then Gillett said, "What's the second thing?"

Andrews turned his face toward Gillett's resting place. "My partner can't abide injustice, be it offered to a stray dog—or a stray Apache chief." Andrews let that sit for a while before adding, "He means no disrespect to you or your mission, Sergeant. And we all know how unlikely it is that the Indians will get to keep their way of life, with the changes happening in this country. But Wiswall doesn't like it. And he won't ever like it. I hope you can understand that, even if you don't agree with it."

"Sometimes hard things have to be done," Gillett said, finally.

"I suppose so," Andrews said, tapping the ashes out of his pipe and lying down on his bedroll. "I lost my mother and father to an Indian attack, so I certainly see the other side of it." As he lay on his back, looking up at the crow's-breast sky, Andrews fingered the gold locket on the chain around his neck. "But, still, even I wonder sometimes … How many wrongs does it take to make a right?"

CHAPTER SEVENTEEN

-

Before sunrise early next morning, everyone was up, their snug bedding folded neatly and packed, the mules re-packed, and the horses unhobbled, saddled, bridled, and ready for the trail. Some of the Rangers had built a small fire and were having coffee and warm biscuits. Talk was sparse and low in the pre-dawn dark, limited to communication regarding the day's journey.

Simon's three brothers and nephew prepared to depart for Ysleta. Andrews and Wiswall surmised that the Tiguas had not slept, instead scouring the Huecos for hidden attackers and then watching through the night. Now they squatted by the fire, eating biscuits and sipping coffee beside the other Rangers. As Andrews and Wiswall watched, Lieutenant Baylor came over and spoke to each one of the men who would leave.

"Thank you, good friends, thank you. I wish you safe journeys home." The four heavily armed Indians stood and each shook Baylor's hand in turn. Simon Olguin clasped each man on the shoulder. Then they went to their ponies and vaulted onto their backs. They reined their mounts out of the firelight; the sounds of their going faded into the dark.

"Home for peaceful sleep," Gillet said quietly, standing beside Andrews and Wiswall. "Too bad the rest of us can't ride back with them."

"Why, Sergeant," one of the other men said, "can't you nap in the saddle?"

"Not today, Seaburn," Gillett said. "Or I might wake up with an arrow in my throat."

"We look and watch or we die," Simon Olguin said as he drank the rest of his coffee. "Like the coyote, like the pronghorn. Like all life on the desert."

A few minutes later, everyone was mounted and ready to decamp. Glancing at Lieutenant Baylor, Simon Olguin rode out first; the rest of the Rangers, with Andrews and Wiswall, reined their horses after him. Day came on without true sunrise, but merely a gradual shading from black into a grudging, dull gray. Clouds lowered threateningly; it looked like a wet day's ride. As they went, the patrol loosened their slickers from saddle packs and slid them on over coats.

"If we ride through the rain, we can make Crow Spring by late evening," Baylor said. "And if those fellows out there, just beyond rifle range, don't get a lot of reinforcements."

Andrews stared hard, as far as he could see, but could pick up no sign of Apache observers. Then Wiswall said, "There. Just right of that far butte."

Andrews looked. Perhaps three-quarters of a mile distant, a mounted figure picked its way along, followed by two more.

"Lieutenant, I've got a Sharps," Andrews said. "They'd be in range for me. Shall I see if I can knock one of them down? I'm told that turned the trick for the defenders of Adobe Walls."

Baylor smiled. "The Sharps … The Indians say it's the gun that shoots today and kills tomorrow. But no." He shook his head. "Simon advises against it. Let them be for now; no need to pick a fight this early in the day. It may come to that, but maybe it won't. In the meantime, we'll ride as though we have no reason to fear or care who sees."

Andrews took his hand off the stock of the Sharps and peered back out over the desert, toward the butte. Now there was no rider visible.

"As bold as brass, we're on our way, boys," Baylor said, raising his voice to carry to the entire troupe. "There will be no forgiveness, reconciliation, or redemption for sloppiness of attention, lack of concentration, or outright recklessness. Let it not be you who fails to focus, leading to our entrapment. If not for your own safety, then for the life of the man riding next to you—pay attention."

They rode along, and once more, Andrews studied the men around him. To a man, they carried themselves as if they were riding through a town park rather than through a bleak desert populated by hostiles. Only their darting eyes betrayed that they were not completely at ease. This is just another day's work for them, Andrews thought.

A cold mist began to sift down on them; soon the horses' coats were slick with moisture—surely not sweat in the chilly air. "Well, at least we don't have to worry about rattlesnakes in this weather," said one of the Rangers, a short, balding, middle-aged fellow named Cloyes. "I'd rather make a bed in the snow than have to worry about a snake crawling into my blankets during the night. They'll do that, you know."

"Ain't a snake this side of the Brazos River that'd sleep with you, Cloyes," one of the other men said. Several laughed at this. Cloyes's face reddened. Andrews heard him mutter under his breath, "All the same. I don't cotton to snakes."

Simon Olguin rode some seventy-five to a hundred yards in front of everyone else. As Andrews watched, he saw the scout's head turn left, watch for a while, then swivel back to the right.

"Three flanking us to the left now, four on the right," Gillett said, riding along behind Wiswall. "And always just out of Winchester range."

"You think they'll attack?" asked Andrews.

"Only if Victorio tells them to," answered the sergeant.

By now they had left the Butterfield trail; Baylor and Gillett had made the decision to cut directly across the desert expanse rather than follow the longer upper trail. They calculated this would put them at the Crow Spring station that much quicker. Also, concealment would be more difficult for ambushers in this open terrain. Of course, that also meant that the Rangers traveled in open view.

"How long have you and the army been dealing with Victorio?" Andrews asked.

"Well, let's see if I can recall the history," Gillett said. "Victorio is chief of a branch of the tribe sometimes called Warm Springs Apaches. In years past, I've heard, he rode with Geronimo, Mangas Coloradas, and maybe one or two others. He and his people were up around Fort Craig, New Mexico, and the order came to move them to a reservation in Arizona Territory.

"Victorio balked, gathered up his braves, women, and children, and lit out for Mexico. This was sometime around the summer of 1877. And for the last two years or a little more, he's been making a nuisance of himself here, in northern Mexico, and eastern New Mexico."

"Looks like the nuisance is growing, Sergeant," a trooper named Fitch said, nodding toward the south. Andrews and Wiswall looked to their right; now there were six braves flanking them, where four had been not long before.

"Our odds are dropping by the minute," Wiswall said.

"So I guess the Mexican authorities would like to see him gone just about as much as you would," Andrews said.

"Oh, I reckon. The milicianos want to see the last of him, too."

The cold mist continued to fall as they rode across the desert, all through the dreary morning. Now and then a jackrabbit would flush from cover in front of them, loping away in zigzags. "If old Shep were with us, we'd have the very devil of a time restraining him," Andrews remarked. Wiswall smiled.

"We ought to raise the Cornudas within the next couple or three hours," Gillett said. "From there, it's still a good thirty-odd miles across to Crow Spring. But we can make it tonight if we ride into the dark."

"I wish it was dark now," Cloyes muttered. "I don't like riding along with them Apaches watching every damned move we make. Pardon the language, Sergeant."

Up ahead, Baylor shouted for Simon Olguin. The scout wheeled his mount and trotted toward the rest of the column. After a quick conference, the lieutenant turned to the others, gathered in a loose semicircle behind him.

"Sergeant Olguin thinks this is as good as any place for a quick rest for the horses and ourselves. It's just about noon, so let's take a half-hour, at most. Seaburn, you stand watch on the left flank, and I'll take the right. Let's give the horses and mules some feed, and eat a little ourselves. Then we'll resume our ride."

As the Rangers began to dismount, Gillett commented, "Our audience is still growing."

Andrews and Wiswall peered out toward the northern and southern horizons. "I make ten on this side," Wiswall said after a few seconds.

"The same, at least, over here," Andrews said.

"Well, better to eat lunch now than in battle formation, I guess," one of the other men said.

"Is Victorio out there, do you suppose?" Andrews said.

"I doubt it," Gillett said. "If he was, we'd likely already know."

After filling feed bags with oats and strapping them on their mounts, the men pulled hardtack and cured beef from their packs and saddlebags and ate while standing beside their horses, washing down the hasty meal with a few swallows from their canteens. Then, as quickly as they had dismounted, they were all back in the saddle and pointed east by southeast.

By this time, Ojos de los Alamos was behind them, off to the left. The party was moving well, despite having to slog through the occasional water-filled washout. They pressed on at a brisk walk or easy trot into the mid-afternoon, and the Cornudas rose up to their left. As the sky began to darken, and with the mist still descending, Lieutenant Baylor called another halt.

"Twenty miles to Crow Spring, men," he said, wincing as he stuck a fist in the small of his back. "Let's feed the animals and ourselves, work a few of the kinks out of our backs and legs, and get ready for the final run."

Dismounting in silence, several Rangers stretched out straightaway on the ground, pulling their hats down to cover their faces. Others tended the horses and mules.

"If they don't come for us before dark, we may at least win clear to the old station," Gillett said to Andrews. "As a general rule, the Apaches don't like to fight at night. Or in the rain."

"Well, then we've got darkness and damp in our favor," Andrews said, trying to shelter his biscuit from the precipitation.

"Why don't you try to get a little rest, Sergeant?" Wiswall said. "I'll see about your horse."

Gillett hesitated a moment, then handed his reins to Wiswall. "I'd be much obliged." He walked off a few paces and stretched himself beneath the bare branches of a cenizo bush.

An hour later, with Simon Olguin riding point, they set out again. Dark had fallen, but still they pressed ahead. At the last fading of the light, one of the men said he counted thirty Apaches in all, about the same number shadowing them to the north as to the south.

"They'll still be out there, even in the dark," Gillett said.

"Well, I'd just as soon not have to look at them, anyhow," one of the men said.

"I just hope we don't have to see them up close," said Wiswall.

Andrews found himself riding beside Lieutenant Baylor, both of them following the barely visible hindquarters of Simon Olguin's pony.

"Unbeknownst to you, Mr. Andrews," Baylor said, "you and your partner picked the very spot for your overnight stay that Victorio and his people know the best. We've realized for a while now that they use the old Crow Spring station on their way south from the Guadalupes toward the country around Fort Davis. It's far enough east, and sufficiently isolated that they don't usually have to worry about being disturbed when they stop there for water."

"Well, I assure you, we had no intention of becoming part of his plans."

Baylor gave a low chuckle. "I expect they were delighted to find fresh horses just outside the station walls."

"I tell you the truth, Lieutenant, they made off with our horses as handily as you please. The hobbles didn't seem much of a deterrent."

"Oh, there's not a thing about stealing horses that anybody can teach the Mescaleros," Baylor said. "It's how they've done business for many a year. They are past masters at the art."

"Their skill was certainly in evidence, much to our disgust. Tell me truthfully, Lieutenant," Andrews continued in a lower voice, "how much danger are we in?"

Baylor rode for some moments without replying. "They seem to be gathering up on our flanks at a great pace," he said finally. "But now at least we have the concealment of darkness—though the noise of our passing tells them a great deal, no doubt. We'll come to the station all right, I calculate. And I hope with all my heart that we find Shep there, waiting for us."

"Yes, as do I, but … It's a long way back to Ysleta, isn't it?"

There was another long pause. "That is a problem for another day," Baylor said at last.

After they had ridden another quarter-mile, Baylor tugged his slicker about him. "The mist has let up, but do you feel how the temperature is dropping, now? It may get mighty cold tonight, especially if the sky clears off. I hope Shep has been able to keep warm enough."

"Well, we left every blanket we could spare in the ambulance and made sure he could get in there if he wanted to."

Baylor nodded. "I expect he'll be all right, then."

"That is my deepest hope, right now," Andrews said. He tugged his hat down, turned up the collar of his woolen coat, and said another silent prayer for the dog that he hoped was waiting for them, somewhere in the darkness ahead.

CHAPTER EIGHTEEN

-

Farther back down the line of riders, Wiswall asked Gillett how much farther he reckoned it was until they reached Crow Spring station.

"If we've stayed on course—and with Simon Olguin leading us, I fully expect we have—we ought to get there within the hour."

The night sky had cleared sufficiently that now they could discern the indistinct cottony shapes of clouds tumbling away toward the southeast, shoved along by a cold wind driving down from the Sacramento Mountains, behind them. Now and then, a patch of moonlight swept across the terrain. The moisture that had been drifting down on them all day, since their departure from Hueco Tanks before dawn, was now freezing on loose-hanging tack and in the horses' manes and tails.

"I never thought I'd be sorry to see it quit raining on me along the trail," Gillett said, "but if it clears off tonight, it will be mighty chilly sleeping weather."

"Not that we'll be doing much sleeping," Wiswall said. "The way it's looking, we may have half of the Apaches in Texas and the New Mexico Territory paying us a visit."

"There is that to consider," Gillett said. "Maybe we can leave again in darkness and be back on the trail to Hueco before our friends out there in the dark realize what we're about."

Wiswall greeted this assessment with a silence that spoke volumes.

"What was that?" Gillett said, suddenly. He sat up straight in his saddle and cocked his head sideways, listening.

"What did it sound like?" Wiswall said. "I wasn't paying—"

The noise came down the wind, faint and intermittent, but present, at the very limit of hearing: a dog barking.

"Shep!" Wiswall spurred his horse forward into a canter, quickly passing the others in the column. He tore past Baylor and Andrews; their surprised faces barely registered as he went by. He quickly bore down on Simon Olguin and then passed him, bearing straight along the line of travel, toward the far-off tumble of the abandoned stage station, barely visible in the intermittent washes of moonlight coming through the scudding clouds.

"That damn fool is liable to get us all killed!" one of the men yelled, just as Andrews kicked his horse forward.

"Shep! I hear you, boy!" Wiswall shouted, urging his laboring mount forward. He heard hoofbeats coming up on his right flank.

"What are you doing?" Andrews shouted, closing to within a few yards of Wiswall and his galloping mount.

"I heard him!" Wiswall called over his shoulder. "Shep! Sergeant Gillett heard him, too!"

"We ought to stay with the others," Andrews hollered.

"You can stay with them if you want; I'm going to get our dog!"

They made all the haste they could squeeze from their nearly spent horses, but the ruined station walls crawled toward them at an agonizingly slow pace. Andrews peered out at the desert landscape as best he could from the back of a galloping horse; if the Apaches were coming after them, he couldn't see any evidence. He hoped his senses were telling him the truth.

When they had nearly halved the distance between themselves and the Crow Spring station, they could plainly hear Shep barking. Despite their fatigue and the bitterly cold wind crawling down their necks, Andrews and Wiswall started laughing.

"Shep, you old rascal!" Andrews crowed in delight.

"Did you save us any bacon, Shep?" Wiswall yelled.

By the time they were a hundred yards away they could see him clearly, perched on the broken wall of the station, jumping up and down on his front legs and barking for all he was worth. After days and days in a desolate, abandoned place—most of it spent with only himself and the lurking coyotes for company—Shep was still there, still waiting for them, still standing watch over the ambulance and the supplies they had left there.

The partners reined their mounts to a stop in the crumbling doorway of the station and clambered down out of their saddles, their cold hands and cramped legs temporarily forgotten. Shep bounded up to them, whining and licking and wriggling like a new puppy. The two men fell on the dog, both exclaiming over him, petting him, rubbing his muzzle and head, his back, his belly.

"He's thinner," Andrews said.

"But he still has some pep," Wiswall said. "If he was in a really poor way, he wouldn't be acting so happy to see us." Shep had not stopped thrusting his nose toward the two men's faces, licking their hands, their cheeks. His tail swung back and forth like a pendulum.

A few minutes later, Simon Olguin rode up, with Baylor beside him. They dismounted and stood, watching the joyous reunion of the two men and their canine amigo. Before long, the rest of the Rangers had gathered up and begun dismounting and leading their horses inside the old station walls. Not a one passed by who didn't grin through his weariness—including the impassive Simon Olguin.

"Well, gentlemen, it looks like your sentinel stood to his post, just as you asked," Baylor said. "You couldn't ask for more faithful duty than that."

"I am sure enough glad to see this old cuss," Andrews said. He couldn't take his eyes off the dog, couldn't stop patting him; neither could Wiswall.

"All right, boys," Baylor called out, "since we have the dog, the Apaches be damned—at least for the next few hours. Let's get the animals hobbled and picketed and get a fire going. The Mescaleros know where we are, so there's no sense in a cold camp tonight."

With Shep padding along between them, Andrews and Wiswall led their horses inside the walls of the station. The ambulance was still there and appeared undisturbed. On the ground underneath the wagon, a very small morsel of the side of bacon they had left with Shep was still visible. The sack of corn was mostly depleted.

"Coyote sign all around," Simon Olguin said, peering at the ground. "Dog kept them away."

"This old soldier had his work cut out for him, that's certain," Gillett said, scratching Shep between the ears. "I declare, it's a marvel, though; you told him to wait, and by gum, he waited!"

"Listen to him!" Baylor said as Shep whined and yipped, still fawning over his owners. "I don't believe I've ever heard a dog utter such sounds before. Fellows, that dog is talking to you as plainly as any animal ever spoke with a human. And I do believe he'd dance on his head, if he could."

Some of the men had gathered enough wood for a good-sized fire and enough dry kindling to get it started; it was beginning to lick up from the center now, crackling and popping as the larger twigs and branches began to blaze. Someone filled the large, tin coffee pot with water from the station tank and set it to heat.

"Put the pack loads in the ambulance," Baylor said. "We'll hitch the mules to it in the morning."

Baylor and Gillett set the watches: three men in two-hour shifts, throughout the night. After a while, bacon sizzled in a pan over the fire. Somehow, the sound and the aroma made the night wind feel less chilly, allowed the still-present danger to recede from the men's minds, ever so slightly.

As the men and animals ate, Baylor reminded everyone to sleep with loaded rifles at their sides. "The Apaches don't usually attack at night, but we can ill afford a surprise," he said.

"Wonder how many of them are out there, now?" one of the men said.

"Reckon we'll know in the morning," another muttered.

Over the next half-hour, most of the clouds disappeared; the moon glowed silver in a sky dusted with stars. Baylor, Gillett, Andrews, and Wiswall hunkered near the fire, huddled in their coats. The two Coloradoans fed Shep from their plates as the dog lay between them.

Wiswall, sipping on his third cup of coffee, said, "Lieutenant, I don't know how we can ever thank you enough."

"Let's wait until we're all back in Ysleta before we start passing out laurels," Baylor said.

Andrews stared around at what he could see of the deserted station by the moonlight. What little remained of the adobe walls was cracked and weathered from top to bottom. The whole place gave the impression that a few solid shoves would topple what structure remained. But if it came to a fight with Victorio in the morning, these crumbling walls would be better than no cover at all.

"What is the history behind this godforsaken place, anyway?" Wiswall asked.

"Well, from what I understand, this station was built about six months after the ones over at Cornudas de los Alamos and Ojos de los Alamos," Baylor said. "The stage line started using them in early 1858. Then, when they switched the route farther south in August of the next year, none of these continued in regular use. Over the next ten or so years, Cornudas and Ojos just about fell to the ground, and the only building left here at Crow Spring was a single structure within this little four-sided enclosure."

A while later, Wiswall said, "Lieutenant, how do you reckon we'll get out of here in the morning? Making the assumption that our escort is still out there, watching, won't it be obvious when we try to leave?"

"Maybe there'll be a fog or a mist to cover our retreat," Baylor said.

Wiswall tipped his head back and studied the jeweled sky, lit by the moon, still riding almost halfway up the western sky. "Fog will have to hurry, I'm thinking," he said.

"Do you know anything about Victorio's history?" Andrews said. "All we know about him is what we've heard along the trail and from you, and none of it has been good. Where did he come from? How did he come to be such a formidable foe?"

Baylor stared at the fire, starting to gutter lower and fall into red coals. "He was born Bidu-ya, I'm told," the Ranger commander said at last. "Supposedly that means 'He who checks his horse.' But as long as I've been out in this part of the country, no one has called him anything but Victorio. From what we can gather, he's getting up some in years, in his 50s by now."

"Impressive that a man can live to be even that old, given his history," Wiswall said in a musing voice.

"He has learned from some of the best," Baylor said. "As a young man, he rode with the war band of Mangas Coloradas, who terrorized much of northwestern Mexico from the 1820s to nearly 1840. Well before the Civil War, Victorio was known to the cavalry and every Indian throughout the southwest as a segundo: second-in-command of the Warm Springs band. Later, he gathered a large number of Mimbreños and Mescaleros under his leadership. With

Cochise and Geronimo, the main Apache chiefs just about ruled this country during the Civil War, when so many troops were withdrawn back east."

"Have you ever seen him in person?" Wiswall asked.

Baylor shook his head. "Only the effects of his passing, I'm afraid. The few whites I've been able to speak with who have observed him up close described him as having a certain gallant air. And I am told that he can be generous and even solicitous with his own people. I'm afraid that I have not observed any evidence of such, however."

A long silence crept past, punctuated by soft pops and crackles from the fading fire. "Well, I suppose we'll know more of his disposition in the morning," Andrews said.

"Something tells me that he'll be here," Baylor said, nodding.

By now, the men not standing sentinel were finding their bedrolls. Andrews stood and went to the Coolidge, where he had placed his Sharps upon arriving at the station. "Make sure your ammunition is dry and at hand, partner," he said to Wiswall, who still sat on the ground, leaning against a wheel of the ambulance as he rubbed a hand up and down Shep's back. "It's likely that we'll have call for it in the morning."

The two partners rolled out their blankets on the ground underneath the ambulance, since the interior was filled with the contents of the mule packs. They made themselves as comfortable as they could; Shep curled up near their feet. Within the space of a half-hour, the Ranger camp was silent and motionless, except for the ceaselessly roving eyes of the sentries.

-

Andrews woke from a fitful sleep to hear a low voice muttering words in a strange tongue, near the place where Shep was lying. He opened his eyes and, moving his head as slightly as he could, he saw the huddled figure of Simon Olguin, squatted on the ground beside Shep, gently scratching the dog's neck and speaking half-whispered words in what Andrews assumed was the Tigua language.

As he watched, Simon's head moved; he was looking at Andrews. As quietly as he could, Andrews eased out from under the wagon and went over to sit on the ground beside Olguin. The Indian's hand never stopped stroking Shep; the dog lay with his muzzle resting on his front paws, his eyes closed. He was clearly relishing the attentions of the Tigua scout.

"Sergeant Olguin, may I ask what you were saying to him?" Andrews said, after a while. "Were you speaking to him in Tigua?"

Olguin nodded, his eyes never leaving Shep. "I tell him a story of his ancestors."

Andrews smiled. "I expect he was glad to hear it. He's likely tired of the nonsense that Wiswall and I chatter to him about, day in and day out."

"I tell him about Coyote, who brings luck for the hunt."

"You hear that, old fellow?" Andrews said, running a palm along Shep's backbone. "You come from lucky ancestors. I'll warrant you've been wondering where your luck got off to, these last few days here, by yourself."

"Many coyotes have been here," Simon said, gesturing about the abandoned station yard. "They could have taken the dog's food. They could have killed the dog, if they wanted to. But they did not.

"They saw that he was their brother. They saw that he was strong-hearted and not afraid. And so they left him alone."

Andrews peered out at the yard, trying to imagine it full of coyotes—watching Shep, smelling the bacon, but not attacking.

"Dog has the luck of Coyote," Olguin said after a few moments. "It keeps him alive." For the first time, the Tigua looked directly at Andrews. "Keeps us alive."

Andrews stared into the scout's eyes for several seconds. Then both of them turned to look at Shep, who still lay as he had, except that now, his eyes were open, flickering back and forth between the two men.

After a while, Andrews returned to his bedroll under the ambulance. Simon Olguin's words were going round and round in his head: Dog has the luck of Coyote … keeps us alive …

Eventually, he slid into a fitful sleep interrupted by dreams of coyotes … circling, circling.

<<line space>>

A few hours later, when Andrews woke, he felt that something was amiss. There was plenty enough light to see, yet he heard no sounds of making ready for departure, nor even the sound of feet shuffling back and forth.

He looked beside him on the ground; Wiswall's blankets still lay there, but he was not in them. Shep was nowhere in sight.

Taking up his Sharps, he cautiously rolled out from under the Coolidge and came up on his knees. The Rangers were all peering out over the tumbled walls of the station. Baylor stood in the center, staring fixedly out past what was left of the station gate.

What was everyone looking at so intently?

With a chill tightening about his entrails, Andrews stood, very slowly, his finger on the trigger of the loaded Sharps rifle.

The station was completely ringed about with Apaches.

And standing in front of the ring closest to the station, plainly visible through the ruined gate, was a man who could only be Victorio.

CHAPTER NINETEEN

For a moment, Andrews wondered if he might still be asleep and dreaming. No one was moving; there were no voices. Each Apache fighter stared fixedly at the station and the Rangers inside, and the Rangers looked at the small army surrounding them, and all was motionless. Even Shep, who sat on the ground beside Wiswall, was as still as if he were a statue of a dog.

Wiswall was standing near Baylor and Gillett, who occupied the near-center of the station yard. Moving as deliberately as he knew how, Andrews went over to them.

"They gathered up before it got light," Wiswall said in answer to his unspoken question. "By the time the sun came up, they were already there. And they haven't moved since— neither has Victorio."

"So ... that is Victorio, then?"

Baylor nodded. "Has to be. The only place any of those braves are looking, other than at us, is at him. He could flick a finger right now, and we'd all be pincushions."

"What do you imagine he intends?" Andrews said. "If he wanted to slaughter us—"

"We'd already be dead," Gillett said quietly. "I have considerable curiosity about his intentions, that's sure."

"Simon? What do you make of this?" Baylor said to the Tigua scout, who stood a few feet away.

"He is watching," Olguin said. "He is thinking."

After a few seconds, Wiswall said, "Let me go out and talk to him."

Baylor whipped around to stare at the stocky Coloradoan. "What are you talking about?"

"Will he recognize a flag of truce?" Wiswall said, already walking slowly, with his hands in plain view, toward the ambulance. "I will go and talk to him. And Shep will go with me."

Now Andrews joined his voice to Baylor's. "Partner? Are you quite sure of your purpose? And your mind?"

Wiswall leaned inside the ambulance, and they could hear the sound of his knife ripping through one of the muslin bags that contained the rations carried on the mules. He sawed off a rough square and fixed it to a long stir-stick from the cooking kit. He stepped out from the ambulance and, in plain view of all the Rangers and the encircling Apaches, he removed his Colt revolver from his holster and laid it on the ground.

"Shep, come here," he said, and the dog, as if he had been waiting for just this word, rose up and padded to stand beside Wiswall.

"Mr. Wiswall, I cannot permit you to do this," Baylor said in a stern voice.

"Respectfully, Lieutenant, I am not asking your permission," Wiswall said. "The only one who can keep me safe right now is the Almighty, and I believe he outranks even yourself. Sergeant Olguin, are you willing to help me speak to Victorio?"

If the Tigua was surprised by this request, it didn't show on his face. He simply walked over to stand beside Shep, facing toward the waiting Apache chief.

"God go with you, William," Andrews said quietly.

Wiswall nodded. He turned toward Victorio, held his white flag high above his head, and walked forward, through the station gate. Shep and Olguin paced him, step for step.

As he walked toward the dour Apache chief, Wiswall told himself to look directly into Victorio's eyes and to show no fear. He had the fleeting thought that it would also be handy to know exactly what he intended to say. God will provide, he thought. And then, he, Shep, and Simon Olguin were standing in front of Victorio.

The chief was broad chested, but not tall—much like Wiswall himself, though less stout. In fact, as Wiswall looked at the older man, he guessed that nothing in Victorio's life would have lent itself to the accumulation of extra body weight. The chief looked like the plants of the surrounding desert: tough, hardy, able to survive where little else could.

His mouth was wide and full; it was set now in a straight line as he looked first at Wiswall, then at Olguin, and finally, for a long moment, at Shep, standing attentively between the two men. Victorio's hair was thick and dark, falling in long, loose locks on either side of his weather-creased face. A red, well-used bandanna circled his head. He wore a simple cotton shirt with a plain front and no collar, and his threadbare, homespun breeches were tucked into leather moccasins with attached leggings that came halfway up his calves.

Wiswall realized suddenly that Victorio carried no weapon other than the long knife in his belt. Of course, the scores of warriors surrounding them were armed with an assortment of bows—each with an arrow nocked to the string and ready to pull. They also carried old Springfield and Enfield rifles, and a few brandished ancient-looking Colt Navy model revolvers.

Victorio was speaking. He paused, and Simon Olguin said, "He says you are one of the men from the wagon who came here alone, with this dog."

Wiswall nodded, keeping his eyes on Victorio.

Victorio spoke again, and Olguin translated, "He says his braves watched you from the time you left Hueco Tanks until you came here. You were not careful with your horses."

Wiswall nodded again. He realized that he was fighting the urge to smile. Keep your tongue in your head until you have something to say, Wiswall, he thought. None of your brash foolishness. Still, the notion that an Apache chief who was, by all accounts, one of the most ruthless enemies the US Army and the Texas Rangers had ever encountered would take the time to lecture him about taking better care of his livestock was so unexpected that Wiswall found himself amused, even though he might not live long enough to walk back to his companions.

More terse words from Victorio. "He wants to know why you have come back," Olguin said.

Slowly, deliberately, Wiswall looked away from Victorio then, kneeling down to pat Shep's withers. "Tell him we came here to get the dog."

When Victorio heard Simon's translation, his eyes widened slightly. He didn't move, but even such a slight variation was notable in such an otherwise stoic face. He said something short, and Olguin repeated it back, nodding once. He said something else, and Olguin said, "He says that he has never seen a white-eye who would do such a thing. He says you must have great power, to make these others risk death for a dog."

"Tell him that everyone who came with me did so by his own choice," Wiswall said, standing up again. "And then, ask him why he thinks it is strange that people like us would show kindness to an animal."

Olguin spoke, and as he did, Victorio's face hardened. Almost before Olguin had finished, the chief was speaking.

The words went on and on, and as Wiswall watched Victorio's face, he fancied he could understand the chief's meaning, though the words themselves were incomprehensible. Finally Victorio stopped and looked at Olguin.

"He says that it was white-eyes who took away the land at Ojo Caliente that was promised to him and to his people," Olguin said. "It was white-eyes who lied to him and who would not listen when his women and children were hungry. It was white-eyes who told him he had to leave his crops half-grown in the fields and go to a place far to the west where he had to make his wikiup in the middle of his enemies. It was white-eyes who killed Mangas Coloradas, even though he came to them under a flag of truce like the one you hold.

"He says that most of the white-eyes he has known have hearts that are black, like meat left too long in the sun. They care nothing for the land, for the other living things, or for the people—only for their bellies. He wants to know what it is about this dog that makes a white-eye think he is worth dying for."

Wiswall stared at Victorio for a long time. The sun was well up by now, and though the air was cold, it did not have the sharp bite that it had held through the bitter night. The breeze had shifted around to the south, and it played around them now, shifting the locks of Victorio's hair and gently stirring the branches of the cenizo bushes nearby. The breeze felt good. Perhaps because he was standing in the shadow of death, Wiswall felt intensely glad to be alive.

"Tell him that the same heart that beats in the Mescalero beats in me and in the rest of my companions," Wiswall said finally. "Tell him that we know what it means to love something enough to risk death. Tell him that this dog is loyal to me, and that means that I am loyal to him: that just as Victorio cares for his people, I care for this dog. And … tell him that if I die because of that, it will be a good death."

Simon Olguin turned to look at Wiswall, and Wiswall nodded. "Tell him. Everything I just said."

The Tigua translated; Victorio's eyes shifted back and forth between Wiswall and Shep. When Olguin finished speaking, it was Victorio's turn to stand silent, carefully studying the face of this man who was saying things that surprised his ears.

Shep chose that moment to step forward slowly, sniff carefully at Victorio's hand, and lick it gently once, then again.

Wiswall would later swear that one corner of Victorio's straight, severe mouth had twitched upward in something that wanted to be a smile. Then he spoke.

"He says that you may die very soon, but it will not be today," Simon Olguin said. "For the sake of this dog, he and his men will let you and the rest of us pass. He says that he is still at war with all white-eyes, but maybe he will not have to kill you or the others who came here with you."

Wiswall sternly counseled himself to keep his relief off his face. "Tell Chief Victorio that I thank him, for myself and my friends. Tell him that I wish there could be peace between us, more than just today. Tell him that I wish that his women and children did not have to find their food in the desert."

When Olguin translated, Victorio spoke again.

"He says that your wishes will not fill the bellies of his people."

Wiswall nodded.

Victorio turned around and walked away a few steps, until he was standing in line with the nearest of his braves. "Enough," he said in English. "You go now."

CHAPTER TWENTY

Wiswall walked back toward the station, where the others waited. He heard Simon Olguin's soft footfalls behind him, and Shep padded along beside. He did not look back. Despite what Victorio had said, his back tingled between his shoulder blades, anticipating an arrow or a bullet from an Enfield.

But neither arrow nor bullet came. He walked back into the station yard, every eye fixed on him. He went up to Baylor and said, "Victorio says we can go. He will not hinder us."

"Is this some sort of joke?" the Ranger commander said.

"It is true," Simon Olguin said, standing just behind Wiswall's left shoulder. "No fight. Because of dog."

Baylor looked out toward the surrounding Apaches, and indeed, they were walking away, Victorio at their head—as if they had seen all they came to see and now had no further interest in what happened. The line of them was angled away toward the place, just on the other side of the old Butterfield trail, where some younger boys waited with the band's ponies. Only a handful of warriors remained in place, observing the Rangers.

"By God, I reckon I can take him down," someone said. Wiswall looked, and one of the younger men was leveling a rifle at the departing back of the Apache chief. He sprang toward the man and slammed the muzzle toward the ground, just as Sergeant Gillett grabbed the Ranger from behind.

"You damned fool! He's letting us go," Wiswall said. "Don't make him change his mind."

"He's right, Allen," Gillett said. "You'd best listen to him."

The man struggled for a moment, but then he relented. He looked around the group, and when his eyes found those of Lieutenant Baylor, staring at him like a hawk studying a rabbit, he ducked away. "All right," he muttered, looking at the ground. "I'm all right, now."

For perhaps two full minutes, the men in the abandoned station watched the astonishing procession in disbelief. Then, as if coming out of a trance, Baylor began giving orders.

"Let's hitch the mules to the ambulance. See that all your gear is in order, and keep your rifles close to hand." Now he aimed a pointed look at Allen. "But do not show them openly or point them in the direction of the Indians; if they truly mean to let us go on our way, we will show them no reason to reconsider."

"What in the name of all that is holy did you say to Victorio?" Andrews said to Wiswall as they gathered their tack and made ready to hitch the mules to the Coolidge.

"Mostly, I listened," Wiswall said, a faraway look on his face. "Shep was the one who presented the majority of our case."

Andrews studied his partner's face, then peered at the dog, who had not left Wiswall's side. "If I didn't know about your gift of blarney," he said, "I'd have more than half a mind to believe you."

Wiswall gave a little smile. "Sometimes a man just needs to say what is on his mind, partner. And then it's a little easier for him to let the other fellow do the same."

"You'll be lecturing in the halls of Congress next, I calculate."

"Oh, no. My gifts of persuasion are wasted on such unrepentant blackguards as those."

Andrews laughed, and it felt good. It was the first time he had laughed out loud since first laying eyes on Shep, the night before.

"We leave immediately, men," Baylor announced. "If we reach the Tanks tonight, we'll break out the fiddles for some refreshing music." He walked over and put his hand on Wiswall's shoulder. "Just about now I confess to feeling a little lightheaded, free for the first time in days from fear and anxiety. I would deeply appreciate your company on at least part of today's ride, Mr. Wiswall, so that you can inform me what witchery you employed to secure our free passage."

"I am happy to ride with you any time, Lieutenant," Wiswall said with a smile. "But I don't know how much my explanation will enlighten you. I'm not certain I understand myself everything that just happened—and I was there."

"I will make you one guarantee, Lieutenant," Andrews said, grinning. "Wiswall can throw a lasso of words around you that will have your head spinning even faster than it is right now. I predict that by the time we've ridden five miles, you will be begging for mercy."

The men saddled their mounts and rigged their gear. Andrews and Wiswall hitched the mules to the Coolidge, now full of the provisions they had brought for the expedition. They smiled and jested; the dark cloud of danger that had hovered over them all was now lifted. The last Mescalero watchmen, apparently satisfied with the Rangers' intention to leave, plodded away across the desert to their waiting mounts; the single-file line of riders in the main Apache band wound behind a small rise and out of sight, no doubt headed back toward the concealing crags and ravines of the Guadalupes.

"Any objection to taking our breakfast along the way?" Gillett called out.

"Hell, no, Sergeant!" one of the men shouted. "Excuse the cussing, but the sooner we put this damned old place at our backs, the better I'll like it!"

Several of the men chuckled. Baylor swung into his saddle, looked around for a moment or two, and pointed out the gate and across the desert, in the direction of Hueco Tanks. He clicked his tongue and put his heels to his mount, and the return journey was underway.

Simon Olguin, as always, took his place well out in front of the rest, and Shep went out to join him, pacing along a few feet in front of Olguin's pony. From his seat on the Coolidge, Andrews grinned and pointed. "Shep always takes point. I hope Sergeant Olguin doesn't mind the company." Gillett, riding beside Andrews, chuckled at the sight.

"Well, sir, I tell you the truth, that was a nervy few minutes back there," Ranger Cloyes said, riding on the other side of the ambulance. "I don't know what your partner said to old Victorio, mister, but I'm sure enough glad he said it."

Gillett, who had just reached for his canteen, now held it aloft. "A toast, my friends," he said, raising his voice to carry all along the line of riders. "To Shep, our savior, and to our two new friends!"

"And a toast to no more of them Mescaleros ready to fill our hides full of arrows!" Cloyes shouted. Everyone within earshot laughed aloud.

With the danger and urgency past, they set a more leisurely pace for the horses, ambling along at a steady walk across the nearly bare, gray terrain of the flats. They had the western Guadalupes at their backs and were aimed toward the distant Cornudas range. The sun's rays were brilliant; an easy south wind fanned them from behind.

By noon, the indistinct, brown outline of a mountain range began to rise on the western horizon, smudged against the crystalline blue sky. "About five or six more hours, I calculate," Gillett said, "and I don't think we'll make Hueco by nightfall. But we can find a likely enough spot for camp in the Cornudas, I'm thinking."

"We're under the wing of old Victorio now, boys," another Ranger said. "No one is going to hurt us. Day after tomorrow, we'll be home."

By the end of the afternoon, they rode into a splendid sunset, arriving in a ravine that cut through the middle of an outlying knoll of the Cornudas. They set quickly about setting up camp and staking the horses and mules, under the watchful eyes of three of the Rangers, to graze for an hour or so among the sparse, curly grass clinging to the chert slopes. Dusk purpled into night as they cooked and ate their travel rations and drank their coffee, taking this meal in considerably more ease than any they had consumed since setting out from Ysleta, days before.

With supper eaten, plates scraped into the fire and wiped with bandanna or shirttail, and smoke from cigarettes and pipes drifting slowly upward in the chilly air, all eyes gradually turned toward Wiswall, sitting cross-legged on the ground between Baylor and Andrews. Shep, of course, was splayed at the feet of the three men.

"Would you favor the men with what you told me on today's ride?" Baylor said into the thoughtful silence. "I believe everyone here would like to know whatever you would care to tell, and for my part, I would certainly not mind hearing the telling at least once more. I suspect this is a story we'll all be telling ourselves and anyone else who will listen, for the rest of our lives, maybe."

Wiswall stared into the fire for the space of perhaps ten breaths, then down at Shep. He reached down and thoughtfully rubbed the shepherd's jaw; Shep's tail thumped slowly on the ground—otherwise, he was motionless.

"I am afraid I can't exactly explain what came over me," he started slowly, sounding like someone telling himself a story he had never heard before. "I was there with the rest of you, looking out there at all those Apaches, every one of them armed and ready for trouble, and a damn sight more of them than there were of us."

"Nothing wrong with your arithmetic, then," one of the men said with a grin. A few low chuckles greeted this remark.

"All of a sudden, the notion came to my mind—from where, I still can't tell you—that for all his cruelty and cunning, Victorio was a man of flesh and blood, just like me … like Lieutenant Baylor, like every one of you.

"I studied on that thought for a bit, and then the notion hit me that I might as well try and talk to him, man to man. He might kill me on the spot, in which case I would have been on hand to hold open the Pearly Gates for the rest of you."

A little more rueful laughter came at this; the men looked at each other and nodded knowingly.

"So, with nothing to lose, more or less, I decided to just walk out there and talk to him. And then, it came to me that I ought to take Shep. After all, he was the reason I was there in the first place, and likely the reason for the rest of you coming along."

"It sure wasn't to save your mangy hide, partner," Andrews said. More laughter erupted.

"So the three of us went out there, while the rest of you watched, likely thinking I'd lost what little was left of my judgment."

"Amen," said Andrews.

"And I wish I could tell you that I knew exactly what I was going to say when I got to Victorio, but that would be a lie. I stood face to face with a man whom I knew could lift a single finger and end my life instantly, and I didn't know what I would say to him—until he asked me why I had come back.

"And that was when I decided to just tell him the truth. We all came back for this fellow, right here." He leaned forward to pat Shep again. "He has been the constant companion of Andrews and me since the day we found him, and we could no more leave him behind than one of you would leave a fellow Ranger. We had to come back for him; that was all there was to it."

No wisecracks greeted Wiswall's pause: only thoughtful looks, deep draughts on smokes, and a few nodding heads.

"And as soon as that thought came clear in my mind, I realized that if anything could change Victorio's mind about whether or not we deserved to live, it was that. Caring enough about a fellow being to put your life on the line … that was something he respected—something he understood.

"I knew he understood that, because that is the same thing he has done."

At this last, a few surprised expressions appeared around the campfire.

"Now, men, don't take me wrong," Wiswall continued. "You are Texas Rangers, and you are sworn to uphold the laws of the state and to protect its people. You don't have much choice about that, and if you weren't willing to do it, you ought not to wear the star.

"But don't you see? Time and the tide of history have put Victorio and his people in a bad pinch. They've been forced off their land and made to move from pillar to post. He's got hungry children that he is responsible for—women who aren't getting enough to eat. I keep asking myself: 'What would I do if my back were to the wall like that?' I think I might be fighting mad all the time, too."

Unnoticed, Simon Olguin had drifted into the far reaches of the flickering firelight. Andrews saw his dim form, standing as still as stone. His face was fixed intently in Wiswall's direction.

"Anyhow, when I told Victorio that I came for the dog— that each one of you came of your own free will, out of sympathy for a good, loyal animal—something changed. I could tell he wasn't expecting to hear that.

"Oh, he's still on the warpath, no question about that," Wiswall said. "If you ride out on his trail next week, it will be 'kill or be killed' when you meet. His anger at his situation is not abated, not in the least.

"But just for today, he saw me—saw each one of you—as men, the same as he is. He saw that some of us white-eyes, at least, have hearts capable of caring for something. And just for today—I'm still not sure why—he decided to let things be different. And that is as much as I can tell you about why we're sitting here right now, smoking our pipes, instead of lying dead or dying back at Crow Spring station."

Andrews looked out toward the place Simon Olguin had appeared. He was still there, but now, barely visible at the edge of the unsteady glow from the campfire, he raised one hand, palm out. It was a salute; Andrews wasn't sure if it was intended for Wiswall or Shep. Maybe it didn't matter.

As he continued to watch, Olguin faded back into the darkness of the desert night.

CHAPTER TWENTY-ONE

By four o'clock the next morning, clouds began rolling in from New Mexico, gradually erasing the glittering stars and dimming the light of the moon that had bathed the Ranger campsite after the fire was coals and ash. By six a.m., the growling of distant thunder was enough to arouse the men, though they were sleeping more soundly than they had since leaving their bunks in Ysleta.

"I knew yesterday's weather was too good to hold," Wiswall grouched, rolling up his blankets and stowing them in the ambulance. "But it would have sure been nice to get back home, at least, before getting drenched again."

"So El Paso is home now, is it?" Andrews said, giving his partner a sly smile. "I thought you had a fiancée you were anxious to get back to."

"You know what I mean."

By the time they had doused the breakfast fire and climbed back into saddles and onto the Cooldige, a slow rain was pattering down. They lined out on the trail, hiding from the shower in their slickers as best they could.

By midday, the worst of the storm had passed; only intermittent drops fell on them as they rode through the afternoon toward Hueco Tanks. They made camp there that night, and despite the damp and cold, the men were cheerful, knowing that they would be back in Ysleta by the end of the next day.

Bernardo, Ponciano, Francisco, and Domingo—Simon Olguin's brothers and nephew—were at the Tanks, waiting for them when they rode in. Baylor greeted them with glad words. "Your brother can tell you about all that has happened to us in the last two days," he said. "It will make quite a story. And I will swear to the truth of every word." Later, Andrews and Wiswall saw the Tiguas huddled in a group, the four listening intently as Simon spoke and gesticulated. From time to time, one or all of them would look over in their direction. Andrews and Wiswall weren't sure if they were studying Wiswall or Shep, who lay on the ground beside them.

"Simon told me a while ago that three Mescaleros were trailing us all day, yesterday," Gillett told them as they sipped coffee by the fire, after supper. "They only turned back when we got here, to the Tanks. He says they were watching us."

"We sure didn't see them," Andrews said.

Gillett shook his head. "I reckon they wanted us to see them on the way out. On the way back, they didn't."

They broke camp at first light the next morning, the men chattering with uncharacteristic animation at the prospect of sleeping in a real bed that night. Toward midday the Ranger party began encountering people working in large, flooded fields, vaqueros moving cattle or horses, loaded ox-carts, and other evidences of the proximity of the town and its comforts.

Near noon, they made a brief halt beside an acequia for a quick lunch from their saddlebags and a chance for the horses and mules to rest and drink. A lone horseman came upon them and halted, staring.

"What is the matter, friend?" Baylor called to him.

"Are you Lieutenant Baylor and the Rangers who went after that dog out at Crow Spring?" the man said, still staring.

"The same, now returning with that valiant dog and the property he faithfully guarded for his owners," Baylor said.

The rider shook his head. "Everyone in town thinks you were all slaughtered. It's all the talk, up and down the street."

A couple of the Rangers started chuckling. "Well, you may assure them that we are not only alive, but almost back home," Baylor said with a big smile. The man rode off toward El Paso, still shaking his head.

"I've always wanted to witness a resurrection," Wiswall said. "I guess that participating in one is even better."

"What do you think, Shep, old fellow?" Andrews said, briskly rubbing the dog's neck. "We've come back from the dead!"

As they resumed their ride after eating, Gillett said, "Lieutenant, when we ride into town, we ought to set Shep up on the wagon seat, so everyone can see him."

"Capital idea," Baylor said. "What do you say, Mr. Andrews?"

"As long as Wiswall doesn't mind either driving the honoree or being his outrider, that suits me fine, Lieutenant."

"It's settled, then," Baylor said. "We'll organize a little parade, in honor of Shep's homecoming. We can even stop at the Osguedo rancho, just down the trail a ways, and paint a sign to hang on the ambulance. 'Faithful Shep,' it ought to say."

And so it was that by early afternoon the troop arrived at the Rancho Osgueda, less than five miles from downtown El Paso. Don Ygnacio himself met them at the front gate of his hacienda.

"Bienvenidos, Capitan! Only yesterday we heard to our deep sorrow that all of you had perished in the desert! And, now, as God wills, here you are, mi compadre! Come and rest, all of you. And especially this perro valiente, who is the cause of such a great adventure!"

Baylor explained that, regrettably, they could not stay long. But Don Ygnacio was only too delighted to have a board and some paint brought from his workshop. Very soon, the Coolidge was adorned with a sparkling white sign with bold red lettering, announcing the presence of Shep, the redoubtable sentinel dog.

Don Ygnacio even insisted on sending along with the party a wagon to carry musicians. "There cannot be a homecoming parade without music," he said. "The bajo sexto and the violín will go with you to announce to the town the return of the heroic dog and his compañeros."

Before much longer, they were on the outskirts of the town. News of their return had preceded them; more and more people were arriving, lining the muddy route, joining the entourage. Shep rode on the wagon seat beside Wiswall, who drove, and Andrews rode behind the Coolidge. Led by Baylor, the Rangers came immediately after, trailed by the musicians; by now, they were busily strumming, bowing, and singing. Andrews thought he recognized the sound of "Trigueña Hermosa," a song popular with the Mexican mine workers back in Colorado. But the words didn't sound the same, somehow. Maybe the singers were changing the lyrics to fit the occasion.

The growing column entered El Paso like a triumphal procession, by now augmented by several dozen children and at least half as many dogs. Though the winter sun was already more than halfway down the western sky, Baylor directed his cavalcade past the canal leading down to the Rio Grande, then left, toward the plaza at the town's center.

People poured out of the buildings on both sides of the muddy streets to see the display. The doors of business establishments opened, and customers, clerks, and owners elbowed each other for a better view and all giving the appearance of wanting to know what the hell was going on.

Once within the large plaza, Baylor led the procession directly to the center; at his urging, Wiswall drove the ambulance right up next to the small pergola, built in a fit of civic pride but now with its paint peeling and a here and there a slat that needed to be nailed down again. The lieutenant dismounted and walked up the steps to the bandstand, then he motioned for Wiswall, Andrews, and Shep to join him there.

Just then, the gathering crowd parted to reveal Sallie Baylor, followed closely by her two daughters. Lieutenant Baylor met them at the base of the pergola steps, and the next several minutes were spent in enthusiastic hugs, tearful greetings, and manly reassurances.

Ascending the steps again, Baylor turned toward the crowd. "Friends, thank you for such a wonderful welcome. These men have ridden far in pursuit of an honorable ideal, and they have come home safely from insurmountable danger. And all of it is because of this dog that you see here, beside me."

He told them the story of how Andrews and Wiswall, unwilling to leave their faithful companion to his fate, implored Baylor for his help. He told about the cold, wet ride to the abandoned station at Crow Spring. And he told of the confrontation with Victorio and its astounding outcome.

"I make no claim to understand the workings of fate or the will of the Divine," he said. "But I do understand faithfulness and courage, and I say to all of you here that this dog, Shep, ought to be known as an honorary Texas Ranger."

The crowd cheered wildly. Andrews and Wiswall looked at each other, grinning like schoolboys.

"I wish we could build a monument to this dog, right here in the plaza," Baylor said. "Such a memorial ought to be inscribed, 'Faithful Shep: a salute to a valiant, noble warrior who leaped into our hearts, and whose blood flows forever with our own.'"

The crowd cheered again, the musicians broke into a joyful cancion, and most everyone in the crowd came up to shake the hands of one or more of the Rangers.

Shep watched it all from his vantage point on the bandstand, his tail wagging vigorously.

EPILOGUE

Andrews hauled back on the lines, and the horses stopped by the gate of the Ranger station. He looked across at Wiswall. "Well, we're here."

"I can't say I'm looking forward to this."

"We can't just leave without saying goodbye."

Wiswall shook his head and climbed down from the Coolidge. Andrews reached behind him and picked up the Springfield he had brought. Shep hopped down and walked between them as they trudged across the yard toward Baylor's house. They walked up the steps onto the broad porch and knocked on the door. The Mexican housemaid opened the door and motioned them inside.

"Yes, you too," Wiswall said to Shep, who hesitated on the threshold.

"Sí, sí," the housemaid said, smiling down at Shep. "El perro es muy bienvenido, todos los días."

"Well, you heard her," Andrews said, grinning at the dog. "Say 'Gracias,' like a gentleman."

"So you're on your way, then?" It was Baylor's voice. The lieutenant was striding toward them, coming from the direction of his study.

"Yes, we'd best be getting on," Andrews said. "But we wanted to be sure to stop by and thank you for … well, for everything."

"I believe I ought to thank you," Baylor said, shaking their hands in turn. "If not for you, I would never have had the honor of meeting this fellow." He kneeled down and took Shep's head in both his hands. "Now, Shep, you take good care of these two, all right? Don't let them go getting into any more trouble." He stood. "I hope you'll take the southern route, this time."

"Oh, yes! Across to Fort Davis, and then back north," Andrews said. "I think we've learned our lesson about taking shortcuts in this part of the country."

Baylor smiled. "And you're sure you won't consider my offer?"

"Lieutenant, I hope you know how honored we both are that you would consider us worthy of joining the Rangers. But I think I can speak for Mr. Wiswall and myself when I say that we have been too long away from our lives and livelihood up in Ouray County. We didn't succeed in our attempt at brokering burros, but we have had an adventure that nothing else in our experience is ever likely to match. And now we feel the need of going home."

Baylor nodded. "I can certainly understand that need."

Now Andrews brought forward the Springfield he had fetched in from the wagon. "Lieutenant, it would be impossible for us to adequately thank you for your courageous assistance to us in our time of need. But as a poor substitute, I want you to take this Springfield rifle. It is in top-notch condition, I assure you; I believe it will give you good service."

Baylor's eyes glowed with pleasure as he took the rifle and examined it. "This is indeed a fine weapon," he said. Then he offered it back to Andrews. "But I couldn't possibly accept this. My men and I were only doing our duty."

"No, sir, I must insist," Andrews said, pressing the rifle back toward Baylor, "you did considerably more than that. You rode into certain danger of your own free will, as did the others. Please, Lieutenant; do not dim my pleasure in this gift by protesting it."

Baylor looked again at the rifle. "Well, Mr. Andrews, if you are sure … This is certainly a generous gesture."

"Yet one that has been well earned, in my estimation," Andrews said.

Baylor shook their hands again. "Well, if you ever have occasion to be back in Texas, you'll always have a place here. And you too," he said, leaning down to pet Shep. The dog licked Baylor's hand and wagged his tail.

When they turned to go, Sergeant Gillett was standing in the doorway. "I heard you were hitting the trail today. I wanted to say my good-byes and see this old fellow here, one more time." He smiled down at Shep. "I wish your partners would leave you with us, Shep."

Shep went over to Gillett and received a vigorous petting. He clearly reveled in it, reaching upward with his snout to lick at Gillett's face. Gillett stood and came over to Andrews and

Wiswall. He shook each man's hand. "I don't expect I'll ever forget the events we've been through together," he said. "If I ever write my memoirs, I will mention our adventures."

Andrews smiled. "Well, Sergeant, you're welcome to make any use of it you wish. I won't ever say anything to contradict or take away from anything you write."

They went outside and walked back to the Coolidge. A knot of men had gathered in the yard, most of them from the party that had ridden to Shep's rescue. Andrews and Wiswall had to slow their progress; each man in the group wanted to kneel down in front of Shep, scratch him behind the ears or along his neck, and say a few words of parting. One or two of the most hardened among them, to Andrews and Wiswall's amazement, even appeared to be choking on their words, swallowing and blinking as they bade farewell to their canine compadre.

Finally, they were back on the ambulance and pulling away from the station. Both men shared the seat, with Shep perched in between.

<<line space>>

"I'm going to miss those fellows," Wiswall said, after they had driven perhaps two miles.

"As will I. And yet, I have the feeling that our affairs will bring us back to Texas, one day. At least, I hope they will."

"Next time, let's pay better heed to the travel warnings we receive along the way."

Andrews laughed.

A slight rise angled upward ahead of them, and they noticed two figures standing motionless at its crest. As the wagon approached, they did not move; it appeared as though they were actually waiting for the travelers. The nearer Andrews and Wiswall came, the higher their curiosity mounted.

"I wouldn't think that highwaymen would stand out in the open, so bold, and announce their presence," Andrews said.

"But just in case," Wiswall said, "I'll have my hand on my Colt, and I'd advise you to do the same."

"I am ahead of you, partner."

And then, Shep's ears flicked forward. His eyes fixed on the two men—as it now became clear that was what they were—and his nose worked busily, sieving the air for their scent. Next, he stood up on the seat, and his tail began to wag, slapping at Andrews and Wiswall, seated on either side of him.

"Well, Shep finds nothing to fear," Wiswall said.

Andrews peered ahead. "By heaven, Wiswall, that is Simon Olguin, standing there! And another Indian with him—one I don't recognize."

The Tigua scout and his companion were as still as statues while Andrews and Wiswall drove toward them. "Hello, Sergeant Olguin," he said when he pulled the team to a halt. "I am glad that we can see you one more time, before we go back to our home."

"This is Itza-chu. He comes from Victorio."

Andrews felt his eyes go wide. One of Victorio's warriors? This close to Ysleta, the army, and the Rangers?

Wiswall found his tongue first. "We are honored that he has come."

"Victorio sent him here under truce to say good-bye to the spirit brother of Coyote, who rides with you."

Andrews and Wiswall stared at each other, then at Shep. Finally, Wiswall said, "Well, Shep. This man has something he wants to say to you. You'd better go talk to him."

The dog peered up at Wiswall and Andrews. "Go on," Andrews said, gesturing with a forefinger.

Carefully, Shep hopped down from the wagon seat. He padded over to the two Indians, first going to Simon Olguin. The Tigua leaned over and caressed Shep's snout, muttering to him in what Andrews and Wiswall guessed was Tigua.

Then Shep turned toward the Mescalero. Itza-chu went down on one knee. He did not touch Shep; instead, he peered intently into Shep's eyes for what seemed like several minutes. Shep stood stock-still, returning the warrior's gaze. Then, Itza-chu laid the tips of his fingers on the top of Shep's head and said a half-dozen words that neither Andrews nor Wiswall understood. He stood and backed up a couple of steps.

Shep, as if on signal, turned and padded back to the ambulance. He climbed back up onto the seat and settled in between Andrews and Wiswall.

"What do you reckon he just said to Shep?" Wiswall said.

"I don't believe we're supposed to know."

Simon Olguin raised a hand; Andrews and Wiswall returned the gesture. Andrews shook the reins and clicked his tongue, and the team leaned into their collars. The ambulance rolled forward.

AFTERWORD

Since the story you have just read is an effort at commingling fictional action and dialogue with historical fact and geography, it is imperative the author reassure his reader as to which personalities and events are the product of history, and which arise solely from the author's imagination.

First, all the characters presented here are based on people (and animals) who actually lived; careful research substantiates their veracity. Indeed, the novel emanates from three paragraphs, a sketch in less than 300 words, reanimating a long-forgotten incident described, among other places, on pages 398–399 in Walter Prescott Webb's classic history, The Texas Rangers: A Century of Frontier Defense, published in 1935.

Years later, speaking of the events from which this story is drawn, Ranger George Lloyd insisted that the survival of the Baylor rescue party was due to "divine grace." Pvt. Oscar Burnes, another Ranger volunteer who usually rode point for the group, claimed the week-long encounter blended, then ignited, an "astonishing human activity between Mescalero Apache Chief Victorio, Captain Baylor, us Rangers, and dog Shep that transcended all credibility." The exact meaning of Burnes's somewhat cryptic description is now impossible to verify, but his words stayed in the author's mind, producing the stream of conjecture that served as the source for this work of fiction.

Such recollections demanded from this writer further explanation, and, if deemed fortuitous, exhumation of as many facts as possible for the story's expansion. Following the first faith, first belief, and first lesson of the first writers of the frontier fiction——"…invented stories, fictitious literature, and figments of imagination can easily have happened in the way you dream them to have happened"—I created a series of chapters endowed with actual personalities in figurative chats and conversations during a special time frame, the intention being to share a noble moment in the long history of other noble Ranger moments.

This story is about larger-than-life heroes: larger-than-life because, as ordinary and unremarkable men hanging around their Ranger post in Ysleta, they in actuality possessed the most admirable of all human traits—the self-sacrificing courage to risk their lives for that of another being, albeit a dog, by entering the heart of Mescalero country during the coldest, windiest, wettest week in West Texas history to fetch and bring home that stranded, hungry animal.

The reader should know that I can find no historical evidence that Victorio and the Rangers ever had the type of confrontation or conversation depicted in the central scene of this book. Nevertheless, I have taken the liberty of supplying it in the interest of the yarn and in the hope that the words exchanged in this imaginary interview might represent some semblance of what these characters would have said in real life, had circumstances been different. I hope that the reader will not only forgive, but actually enjoy, this flight of fancy on my part.

Because of men like J. W. Seaburn, John Thomas, J. P. Miller, George Lloyd, R. M. Head, J. N. Garcia, D. B. Fitch, A. J. Cloyes, Oscar Burnes, J. L. Allen, J. B. Gillett, G. W. Baylor, J. W. Andrews, W. P. Wiswall, and Tigua Indian scout Simon Olguin with his three brothers and nephew, Shep still lives. He is everywhere, in every dog. Just look into the eyes of your own, and you'll see him.

WHY THE RANGERS WENT TO CROW SPRINGS

By

Chuck Parsons

One might say that a man will do dangerous things for friends; some might say men will do not only dangerous but even foolhardy things. Why? For no reason at all, or for the thrill, or for spite, or for some other nondescript reason that that the man himself cannot explain. The fictional gunslinger Frank Morgan, in the 1995 motion picture Gunfighter's Moon, admitted that sometimes he did strange things but could not explain why. Is man the only one of God's creatures who does things for an inexplicable reason? We would suggest not, and perhaps the concept of fidelity somehow enters into the picture. Suggesting that fidelity and mankind are two agreeable entities may be subject to mockery by some. The pessimist will quickly remind us of several of the most notorious characters of history: Benedict Arnold, Judas Iscariot, and Marcus Brutus.

But there are also examples of fidelity from the pages of history. One thinks of the feelings of David and Jonathan; the enduring love of Romeo and Juliet; the fidelity or love of a Lassie for her master. There exist such creatures – both human and animal – that will not only remain faithful but if necessary sacrifice their life for a friend. But in the context of the above there are feelings, such as love and affection for another, which can be returned by the other. What about love or fidelity for something that cannot return that same affection, such as an inanimate object, or an idea, a concept? One heroic example comes to mind: on a makeshift gallows, Nathan Hale complained of having only one life to give for his country. Even in the twisted mind of John Wilkes Booth his was an act of sacrificing the life of a president for the love of his defeated country.

The love of country certainly reflects fidelity, but in the barren sands of a desert a man can ride and let his mind wander as to why he is there in the arid waste and danger. A man can be alone with his thoughts, ever mindful of a star on his chest, a badge symbolizing his devotion to the call of duty. The star represents his love for law and order; his devotion to his territory or state, his willingness to defend not only law and order but his oath, his word of honor. In Canada, perhaps these are the thoughts of a member of the Royal Canadian Mounted Police. In Texas it is the Texas Ranger, heir to a history of over two centuries that holds the memories of men who fought not only for the most elemental thing – self-preservation – but also for the dignity of the star. The essential Texas Ranger would not tarnish that badge, but as in any profession, there are those who forget that purpose. In such cases, one like Capt. John R. Hughes or Capt. Bill McDonald or Capt. Frank Hamer – highly honored men in

Ranger history – becomes instead a Sgt. Baz Outlaw, letting the love and need for alcohol overcome him, ultimately allowing his fidelity to booze overcome all else. Instead of being placed on a pedestal of honor, beloved and admired by those he saved and protected, the name of such a one becomes a synonym for failed glory.

The lawman, and in today's society, the lawwoman, lives every moment on the edge, never knowing if a "simple" arrest may turn deadly or if the routine traffic stop may turn into a gunfight. A domestic dispute or family argument, once an officer enters to protect an abused wife or child, may turn into a life and death situation between the officer and a violent husband or boyfriend. Why does a person take this risk, this chance of becoming a victim instead of an "ordinary" hero? It certainly is not because of a monetary reward at the end of the day. It is almost certainly not because of the act resulting in an ego boost, although that sometimes may enter into the picture. Could it be nothing more complex than that the officer, having sworn an oath to uphold the law, feels compelled to follow that strand of honor, of faithfulness to the badge, like the *cinco peso* badge that was so common among Texas Rangers of the nineteenth century?

James Buchanan Gillett was just one of perhaps 100 young men who joined that law enforcement group which has become world famous. In the 1870s, when he was a member of the Frontier Battalion, he was attracted to the life of the great outdoors, the fresh air and cool water in streams, and also the thought that possibly there would be a chance to see action against an Indian marauding party. There was action to be lived. He was young, and the thought of being killed in action perhaps never came to him. He certainly faced danger in every arrest he made. He took his life in his hands every day; even in camp he could not be totally safe, as there was no quitting time for a Texas Ranger. From sun up to sun down and all through the starry night there was danger. It might be only an arm's length away.

As one of those who lived through the danger, he occasionally may have wondered: Why am I doing this?" If so, his answer might have been nothing more complex than that it was duty, an obligation to do what was right, to protect life, whether the life of a horse, a dog, or a fellow Texas Ranger. Honor is not a tangible thing, but it is something that a Ranger is proud to bear, and to silently know that his actions have saved the life of a creature, one of God's creatures, may have been enough. That untarnished badge will not bring about wealth or fame, but it will provide a strong feeling of contentment in the soul.

Chuck Parsons is a prominent Texas historian who writes often about the Texas Rangers. A frequent contributor to True West Magazine, his books include John B. Armstrong, Texas Ranger and Pioneer Ranchman; "Pidge," Texas Ranger; The Sutton-Taylor Feud: The Deadliest Blood Feud in Texas; and Clay Allison, Portrait of a Shootist

MEET THE AUTHOR

Don DeNevi

Don DeNevi was born in Stockton, California, where his father ran a hardware store. Seeing the Stanley Kramer film "My Six Convicts" at the age of 14 incited a life-long fascination with the psychology of imprisonment and the viability of rehabilitation. In the late 1950s, he interned as a teacher at a prison near Stockton before graduating from San Francisco State University with a B.A. in History. He continued his education at U.C. Berkeley, from which he received his Ph. D in the early 1970s, and has since taught classes such as Criminal Profiling, Organized Crime in America, Classic Crime Cinema and Understanding the Criminal Mind at multiple colleges throughout the Bay Area. The author of dozens of books, Don is a prolific writer and a fan favorite for many readers.

THANK YOU FOR READING!

If you enjoyed this book, we would appreciate your customer review on your book seller's website or on Goodreads.

Also, we would like for you to know that you can find more great books like this one at
www.CreativeTexts.com

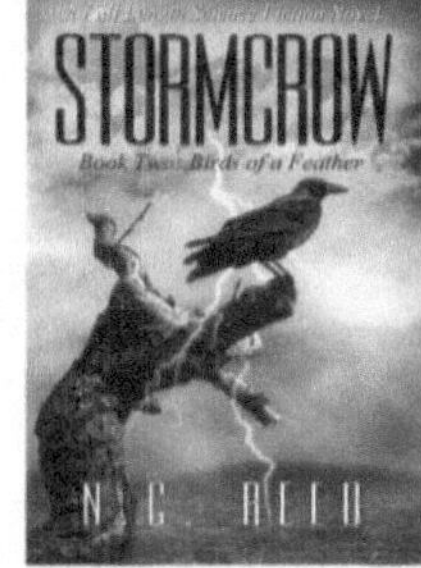